His Sweetheart

THE SAINTS || BOOK TWO

A. Alatorre & A.Smith

ISBN (Print): 979-8-218-39305-2
ISBN (Ebook): 979-8-218-38477-7

Excerpt From
HIS SWEETHEART
A. Alatorre & A. Smith

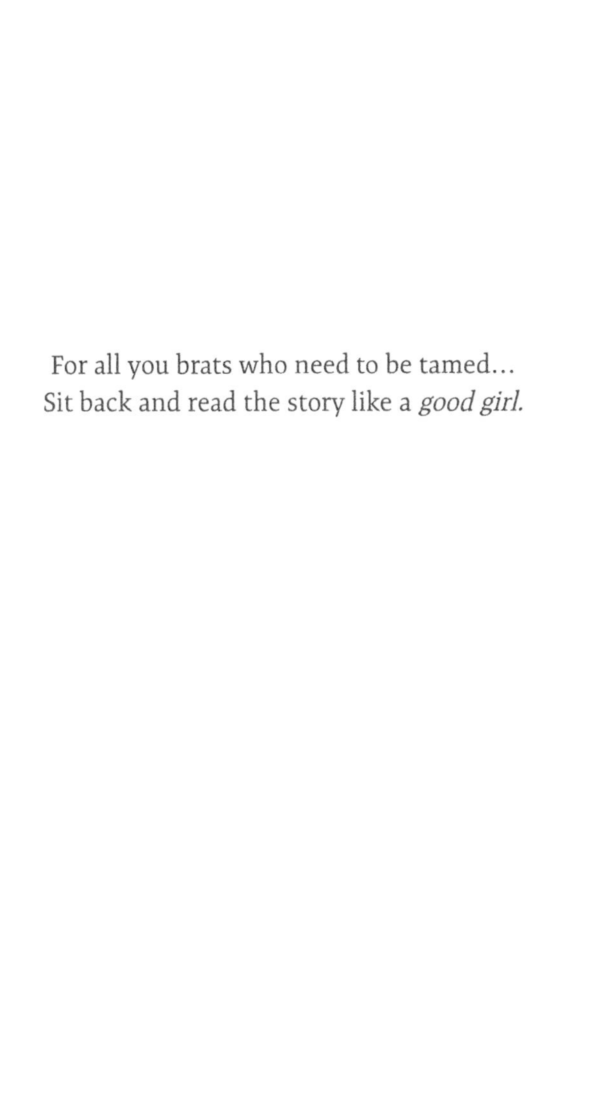

For all you brats who need to be tamed…
Sit back and read the story like a *good girl.*

Pronunciation Guide

Deyanira -(DAY-uh-near-uh)
Bichito -(Bi-chi-toh)
Alessandra -(A-les-an-dra)
Lykos -(Lee-kos)
Erebus -(AIR-eh-vaws)

His Sweetheart

Spotify Playlist

Prolouge

THE WINE

UNKNOWN

A heavy knock rapping against the cracked door alerted the woman of the man's presence. She sat behind her desk, gazing out the large antique windows, a glass of dark red wine in hand. He paused for a moment, out of respect, before cautiously entering the office. Stopping before the desk, the man fidgeted with a thick file tight within his grasp. "We found them," he paused, "but there's a problem." The words fell from his mouth, tainted with nervousness as he reached his arm out, extending the file in her direction. The woman held out a well-manicured hand, her deep, matte burgundy colored polished fingers gripping the thick file.

The room sat in a heavy silence as she flipped through the many pages, broken only by a gasp of disgust. The woman squeezed her hand, the wine glass shattering within her palm as the man flinched by the sudden aggression. Blood and wine mixed together as it ran down the woman's hand soaking the large citrine stone center of her golden ring, held between the teeth of two snarling wolves encrusted in chocolate diamonds, a representation of her position. The man hesitated before whipping the handkerchief from his pocket, his hand shaking as he motioned it in the woman's direction. She snatched the light colored material, cleaning the blood and wine from her hand.

Chapter One

THE CATHEDRAL

V

The smell of grease filled the air as I stepped from the car and approached the restored gothic structure of one of my personal favorite organizations within the Saints, the Cathedral. The sun peeked from above the pointed spires of the converted building, causing me to squint as I admired the structure. *Leave it to The Saints to transform an old, European-style church into a high tech mechanic shop.* I chuckled at the impressiveness of the building, reaching into my leather jacket as I unwrapped a heart-shaped sucker and made my way around the back to the garage entrance of the Cathedral.

The sound of clanking, metal scrapping, automatic tools and distant heavy metal music played as I turned the corner, the garage doors pulled open as mechanics worked on various cars and parts. The shop was huge, stretching the full length of the Cathedral. A partially tattooed man stood outside the shop, phone in hand as he seemed distracted, unaware of my existence as I neared him.

"Long time no see, Diggs." I smirked, the sucker clenched between my teeth. Diggs popped his head up, forcing a smile as he held a finger up motioning me to his office. I nodded, making my way into the shop, taking my sweet time.

My curiosity got the best of me as I dawdled through the spacious garage, observing the various projects and parts, as well as the wide variety of the cars the mechanics were working on. A navy blue muscle car caught my attention as I approached the back of the car, my eyes scanning the smooth shine of the paint job, admiring the white leather interior as they landed on the propped hood. Whistling, I admired the craftsmanship of the white leather interior, as my sight landed on the propped hood. I strolled to the front of the car, my interests piqued, to catch a glimpse of what was under the hood when the sight of another beauty caught me off guard.

I couldn't help but smile as I took in the sight of her from her worn work boots, the dirty coveralls tied around her waist, the rough material pulled snugly over her juicy, peach-shaped ass. She wiped her forehead leaving a smear of grease, beads of sweat running down her neck and reaching her breasts as her tank top clung tightly to her skin. Her black, magenta, and purple-dipped hair was pulled high above her head, stray hairs lightly hiding her cognac-colored eyes as they shifted to meet mine. Her sparkling eyes widened in surprise at the sight of me as she quickly pulled her headphones from her ears, her hands covered in grease.

"If it isn't my favorite Hart sibling." I barely leaned against the side of the hood, winking. She withdrew her body from beneath the hood, flashing me an annoyed look as she slammed the car hood barely missing my arm. *Still feisty.* The bratty attitude made me smile. "Aren't you just a sweet peach." She rolled her eyes, grabbing a small hand towel, wiping her dirty hands

"What the fuck are you doing here, V?" She crossed her arms and tilted her head. "And my name's Hart, not Peaches."

"Come on now, you used to love it when I called you Peaches." I teased, leaning back against the hood of the car. "Admit it," I pulled the heart shaped sucker from my mouth, "you missed me."

"Sorry to disappoint you, but you can't miss what was never there," she snapped, turning away.

I grabbed my chest, offended by her words. "Well, now you're just being rude." I placed the sucker back in my mouth, shadowing behind her as she walked away.

Hart whipped her head, stopping me as we stood close, my eyes looking down at her. "What are you even doing here? This is for employees only." I withdrew the sucker as I stared down at her. She grabbed the heart-shaped candy and dropped it to the floor, stomping on it with her work boot.

"No food in the shop, you know the rules." She pushed past me with force.

My smile remained, entertained with her behavior, turning to face her. "Aren't rules just made to be broken?" Her eyes met mine as I winked.

"V," Diggs called from the foot of the stairs that led to the office above. Hart turned away, returning her headphones to her ears as she shook her head in aggravation. I stuffed my hands in my pockets and approached Diggs. As I moved to step past him and headed up the stairs, Diggs reached his arm out and gently stopped me. "V," he sighed, "I know you and my sister have history, but leave her alone." Our eyes locked as my hurtful past played in my mind. "The Cathedral can't handle another 'remodel'. Took us weeks to handle the aftermath last time."

THE VELVET STAG

My hand knocked against the open door before stepping into Nicholas's office of the Velvet Stag. "Boss man." Nicholas glanced up at me from behind his desk. "I got that intel you requested," I removed the heavy file from beneath my jacket, "but there's more than we expected…and it's a bit concerning."

Nicholas eyed me, closing his laptop as he leaned back in his chair. "Explain." opened the thick file. "Well, aside from your requests, Diggs voiced a concern about something pretty significant." I began placing images of buildings and businesses across his desk. "It seems that some of our Havens have gone silent." Nicholas leaned forward, eyeing the various images.

"You don't think the Lykos family is responsible, do you?" Nicholas quickly asked, glancing up at me.

"Diggs has already begun monitoring known members of the Lykos family, among other known members of opposing organizations." I pulled a sheet from the file and slid it in his direction. "After discussing some options with him, we decided that it might be best to investigate this issue in person. I took the liberty of assigning Keepers to the different Haven locations." Nicholas scanned the sheet of paired names and locations stopping as his eyes met mine.

"I see you chose Angel to visit the Kings, and it looks as though you assigned yourself to the Cathedral?" His eyebrow raised. "Interesting choice there, V."

I couldn't help but smirk at his words, lightly nodding. "I do know the place pretty well."

Nicholas shook his head, examining the information before him. "Just stay out of trouble, V."

"You know I can't promise that," I teased. Nicholas sighed, knowing I was right.

"And the other intel?" he asked, stacking the paper and photos.

"After everything with Theo," I placed the open file and remaining information on his desk, "Diggs scoured his background. Turns out your Vixen's connections to this world are more than we expected."

Nicholas raised a brow as his eyes scanned the intel. "Interesting."

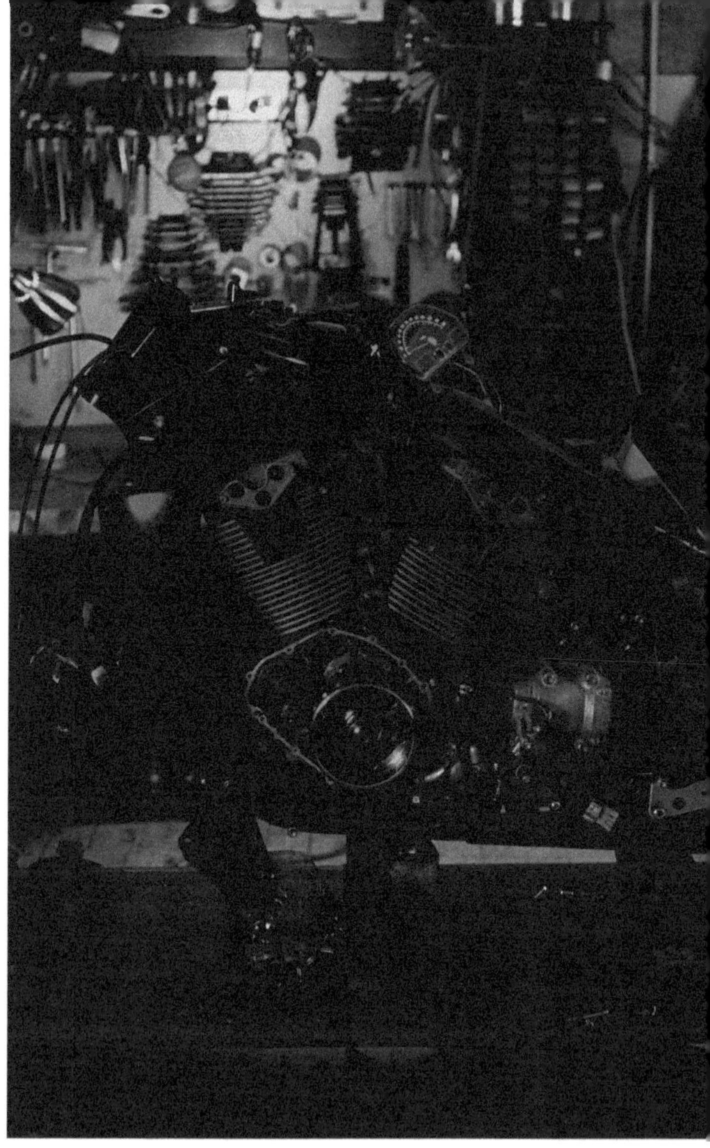

Chapter Two

THE LEASH

HART

The Cathedral was cold, the crisp night air still lingering as I walked to the front of the shop and pressed the roll-up button. The garage doors slowly began to lift, the sound of metal lightly scraping as they fully opened. I glanced out the lifted automatic doors to find V standing just outside, grinning like a child. *Are you shitting me?*

"Morning, sweet cheeks." His long, dirty blonde hair was pulled up into a bun atop his head, his tattooed hand rubbing his beard as he stood just outside the shop. He wore his favorite leather jacket, a simple t-shirt that only enhanced his muscles, and weathered jeans that I just knew clung to his ass cheeks. I shook my head, pushing the thoughts of him from my mind as I crossed my arms.

"What the hell are you doing here?" I tilted my head. "Did your owner finally let you off the leash?" I couldn't help but smirk at the insult, pleased with myself.

V's grin remained as he stepped forward, towering above me. "Since when do you not like leashes?" The heat from his words fell softly against my face as his dreamy blue eyes gazed down at me.

My cheeks burned as I fought back my feelings and remembered our past, my smirk quickly disappearing. "Since I was bit by a *mutt*," I snapped, turning my back to him. I pointed to the stairs that led to my brother's office and spoke over my shoulder. "Diggs is upstairs, go bug him." Before he could speak, I pushed my headphones in my ears and began blaring music, drowning him out.

V

Stopping at the base of the stairs that lead up to Digss' office, I turned looking back at Hart. She always hid her emotions well, but I could see straight through the facade. The distant look of pain and hatred in her eyes had only made her words cut deeper. She meant what she said. I forced my gaze from her, making my way up the stairs. I inhaled deeply, shaking the surreal moment from my mind as my fist knocked against the office door before entering.

"Yo, Diggs!" I resumed the cheery persona. "Where are you at?" I playfully forced the words as I pulled a bright red sucker from my jacket pocket, popping it in my mouth. The stairs lead to a spacious office that stretched a way back into the Cathedral, lined with large tinted windows that overlooked the entire shop below. Playing with the sucker, I stepped toward the wall of glass and watched as mechanics worked. The sound of muffled music and tools clanking amongst distant voices bled together, but one voice stood out. My eyes instantly fell to her as she laughed, her smile intoxicating. I couldn't help but smile, watching as she jokingly flipped off another mechanic.

"Over here, V." Diggs' voice pulled my focus from the window as I stepped around the corner.

He was sitting in front of a wall composed of numerous monitors and screens, each shining brightly with a different image or browser. It was an overwhelming presence of technology clashing the mechanic side of the office. His knowledge of technology and years of assisting the Saints with intel had made Diggs an extremely valuable asset. It only made sense that he would be the head of Nicholas' intelligence and a part of the Keepers.

"Just wanted to give you a heads up that based on your intel, Nicholas agreed it was best to assign Keepers to the Haven locations you mentioned. He wants us to keep an eye on everything, make sure no more locations go quiet." My eyes moved from the various monitors. "That being said, you're going to be seeing alot of me around here."

Diggs sighed, shaking his head before spinning his chair to face me. "No offense, V, but why weren't we assigned someone like Angel?"

I smirked, holding back my emotions. "Angel is being sent to handle something a little closer to home. Besides," I pulled the sucker from my mouth, twirling the red heart candy between my fingers, "we both know I know this place better than the other Keepers."

"Too well," Diggs scoffed under his breath. He cleared his throat, accepting his orders. "Shit. Well, if you are going to be hanging around here, we need to set some ground rules."

I returned the sucker to my mouth, plopping down in an empty chair next him, spinning once before leaning back as I propped my feet atop his desk, crossing my legs. "We all know how I feel about rules, Diggs." My arms reached behind my head as I lounged back.

Diggs remained still, obviously tense. "Val." The serious tone of his voice melted my playful attitude, alerting me to the severity of his concerns. "Look, I want to keep Hart out of this, *all* of it. I don't want her involved in any of it—the Keepers, the Havens," he lightly tilted his head raising an eyebrow, "or you."

"She is just as much a part of the Saints as we are, Diggs," I trailed off.

"Not by choice. Please, V."

I knew he was trying to keep his sister safe, but something told me this was not going to end well. Hart was smart, and knowing her the way I did, I knew it was only a matter of time before she started to ask questions. I leaned forward, hands clasped between my legs as my eyes remained low, my voice tainted with irritation. "Keeping your sister safe is one thing," I peered up at Diggs, "but I won't lie to her." *Not again.* "If she finds out I am keeping things from her, lying to her, there will be *nothing* left—" The words drifted from me, fading as I spoke.

"Nothing left?" Diggs retorted with an exacerbated laugh. "I hate to break it to you, V, but you made sure of that all on your own last time."

The painful truth of his words stung. My chest began to tighten, my hands now gripping the arms of my chair, forcing my face back to a cool mask of indifference. I forcefully hid the impact his words had made. Before Diggs could notice my white-knuckled grip on the chair, his phone rang, playing an unexpected song: Crazy in Love by Beyonce.

The unexpected song broke the tension as my usual smirk returned to my face. "That's an interesting ringtone you got there, Diggs."

Slightly embarrassed, he quickly grabbed his phone and swiped to answer the call. A muffled feminine voice spoke from the other end, accompanied by the now blushing Diggs. Moving the phone from his face, Diggs' attention returned to me. "I have to take this." I nodded, standing from the chair understanding my cue to leave as Diggs whispered into the phone.

Leaving the office I made my way down the stairs and back into the lively shop. I scanned the various muscle cars, my sights halting on a weathered tarp located at the back of the shop. My curiosity grew as I moved closer to inspect what the tarp was hiding. My hand reached out lifting the corner of the vibrant blue plastic to reveal the back end of a motorcycle. In one tug, I whipped the tarp away revealing a motorcycle I didn't expect to see again. Squatting down, my eyes trailed along the bike as my hands moved lovingly across the black leather seat as old memories played in my mind.

"No, you have to keep your eyes closed." My palms remained over Hart's eyes as I led her to the surprise I had planned, leaning in as I whispered in her ear, "trust me."

"Val, I'm going to fall," she joked, slightly nervous.

My hands gently pulled her back, pushing her body against my chest. I shifted my left hand to cover both her eyes as my right arm trailed downwards, wrapping around her waist. My fingers grazed over a small strip of her light honey, exposed skin. "I got you, Sweetheart, always." My words fanned over the shell of her ear, my close breath causing her cheeks to flush as her skin began to pebble with goosebumps. Letting my words sink in, I dropped my left hand from her face to reveal a matching pair of matte black, Indian motorcycles.

She released an audible gasp. "Val, you didn't." Hart pulled away, unable to resist the beautiful bikes as she ran her hands along the sleek body, noticing the small custom design stitched into the leather seats—a pair of pink *hearts, joined together with an arrow, stitched into the matte black seat.* "Val," she whispered, "this is too much." She turned, staring at me with tears brimming her beautiful brown eyes.

"For you, Sweetheart, nothing is too much."

With a swift sudden nudge to my side, I landed hard on my ass as reality snapped me back. I glanced up, my brows furrowed only to meet Hart's rage filled eyes locked on mine, burning into me. I cautiously tried to move, only to land back on the cold concrete as Hart yanked the tarp out from under me with such passion.

"What the fuck do you think you are doing?!" she growled, turning as she covered her motorcycle with the tarp, tucking it away like our past.

Remaining on the floor of the garage, I tried to mask my feelings in humor. "The dust on that beauty tells me she's been neglected." Seeing her old bike had brought everything I tucked away back to the surface.

Hart scoffed, crossing her arms. "Because you're *such* an expert in recognizing when something is being neglected, right?" We sat in silence for a moment before Hart turned, facing away from me as she whispered her words under her breath, "You said always." I knew she didn't think I heard her, but I did. *And I meant it.*

Quickly standing to my feet, I closed the distance between us, invading Hart's space, the sudden movement startling her. As she tried to move away, I lightly gripped her chin between my thumb and forefinger, forcing her attention back up at me as I stared into her eyes.

"I know I've caused you pain," she glanced up at me, listening as I spoke, "but decisions were made… They weren't easy, but they had to be done. You know that." She tried to move from my grasp as I held her firm. "And I know my actions hurt you, but, *Sweetheart*," I softly smiled, "don't think for one second that I don't have regrets. The reality of losing you haunts me every damn day." My face leaned close, our mouths almost touching as our breaths touched. "I fucked up. And every day since… I—" I was too mesmerized by her b eautiful eyes as she sat, waiting for me to finish my sentence. But I couldn't. Sighing, I released her chin as her head fell. *I can't do this now.* I clenched my fists at my side. "I-I have to go." Lowering my eyes as I left, I turned on my heel. I could feel the heat of her gaze on my back as I walked out feeling like my tail was firmly tucked between my legs. *What have I gotten myself into?*

Chapter Three

THE DATE

HART

My body leaned over the workbench as I mindlessly scrubbed my tools, struggling to forget my interaction with V from the day prior. The music in my earbuds blared as I attempted to drown every thought of him out. I didn't need this, not now.

Distracted, a light tap on my shoulder startled me as I turned to see Diggs standing next to me, his mouth moving but his voice drowned beneath the screaming music. He cautiously removed one of my earbuds so that I could hear him, the sound of the lively garage returning.

"You know, if you keep scrubbing like that, there won't be much of that wrench left to work with." He forced a soft smile, noticing my unchanged face. I snatched my headphone back, turning my focus back to the workbench.

"You need something?" My voice snapped immediately regretting my tone. I wasn't trying to be a bitch, at least not to him, but I just wasn't in the mood to deal with anything right now.

"Just wanted to let you know I'm heading out for a bit." I nodded, my face still turned from him. "Oh, and, Hart?" He cleared his throat. "Heads up." I turned to look at Diggs as he lifted his arm up pointing over his shoulder with a face. My head tilted, peering around him to see V. He was dismounting his bike, dressed in his casual attire, smiling as he began to step in my direction. Diggs patted my shoulder. "I'll talk to him."

"Thanks," I grumbled as he approached V. I tossed the dirty rag across my shoulder as I pulled my phone from my coveralls, pausing the song and frantically searching my playlist for something—anything that would silence my thoughts. Diggs and V's voices were low as they whispered. My finger hovered over the playlist when I caught a piece of their conversation. The familiar names caused me to linger close by.

"Yeah, last I heard Angel had reached the King's Haven, but things have gone radio silent since. I'm expecting a call soon. I'm sure everything's fine. I mean, it's your girl Angel. You know she can handle anything." Diggs sounded confident.

V's gaze fell on me, weighing heavily before he shifted. The following words came out quiet and clipped, "Keep me updated. Nicholas will want any additional information you find immediately." *Fucking Nicholas.* Rolling my eyes, my body turned back toward the workbench, not caring enough to continue listening. Pretending to not have heard their conversation, my finger tapped the playlist, scrolling as I shifted to return the phone safely to my coverall pocket. Unfortunately, the phone slipped from my grease-covered hand, landing face down on the concrete with a loud crunch. *Shit.* My body froze, pausing as I slowly turned and locked eyes with a smirking V.

I lost myself in the music for what felt like hours following the earlier incident, annoyed with my now cracked phone. My stomach rumbled loudly as my eyes glanced toward the clock realizing I haven't eaten all day. Removing my earbuds, I turned towards the sink, intent on washing up before eating when a quiet, familiar voice singing stopped me. My attention followed the faint voice as it carried me to the other side of the shop to find V sitting with his back to me. He seemed to be messing with his motorcycle, annoyed with something.

"What the hell... I *know* this is where it goes," V hissed as he tossed the tool aside, the metal clanking as it landed on the concrete floor next to a pile of miscellaneous tools. "Damn it!" V examined a small part from the bike before setting it on the floor. "One missing piece won't hurt." He lightly chuckled.

I moved without hesitation as I approached him, standing directly behind crossing my arms. "You're doing it wrong," I barked. V briefly glanced over his shoulder, eyeing me as his focus returned to the motorcycle and he continued tinkering. A low groan escaped my mouth as I squatted down, shoving him over, "Here, give me that before you break something." I removed the tool from his hand, adding it to the ridiculous pile between us. I extended my hand, waiting for the small part he discarded. V seemed unaware of what I was asking for as I snapped my fingers at the small piece next to him. Placing the part in my palm, the warmth of his hand caused me to pause. My eyes glanced at V, the realization of how close we were, causing me to lose my words. He remained turned away from me, his wild, dirty blonde hair falling loose from his signature top knot as it framed his face, the sun peeking from the open garage as it highlighted his profile. As he slowly turned to face me, his dreamy, bright blue eyes sparkled. He flashed me a warm smile that melted my walls. I soaked in the moment before becoming aware that I, too, was smiling. The tension between us crackled as my gaze slowly trailed from his eyes to his lips. V moved, gently closing the distance between us. My body instinctively leaned in as my right hand reached high, delicately brushing a long golden stray hair from his face. He reacted to the warmth of my touch, sharply inhaling as his heavy lids fell shut. The overbearing urge to touch him, to move closer, increased. My body suddenly wanted him, *craved* him. I slid my foot forward accidentally knocking the pile of scattered tools, jumping as the loud commotion effectively broke the trance.

I quickly dropped my hand, clearing my throat before settling back on my heels. *What the fuck... Focus.* Forcing my attention back to the motorcycle, I gently guided the part into place without looking V's way. I glanced around, searching for the needed tool when I noticed the socket was just out of reach on the other side of him. *Of course.* "Hand me that socket wrench," I snapped, avoiding eye contact. V sat for a moment before gently setting the tool in my extended palm. My arm twisted, tightening the piece into position. I scanned the body of his bike noticing that nothing else was missing or in disorder. Placing my hands on my knees, I stood only to feel a light brush of V's fingertips on my bare arm. My body reacted, quickly moving as I forced the necessary distance between us.

"Breaking things already?" Diggs thankfully interrupted the moment as he strolled over to us.

"Nothing I can't fix." V smirked.

"Well, as fun as this is," I motioned to the three of us, "I have places to be and people to meet." I began to pivot toward the stairs, heading off to clean myself up, when V's voices carried through the garage.

"What does that mean?" V questioned from behind.

"Didn't you know?" I twirled, grinning. "I've got a hot date tonight" I winked, remarking snidely.

V

I shut the tool box, slightly angry, making my way over to the workbench where

Diggs was standing. "Yo, Diggs," his eyes drifted from his phone and met mine, "what's the story with this *date*? Who's the guy?" Diggs sighed, crossing his arms over his chest. "It's still pretty new. They have only met up a few times over the last couple weeks, but she seems happy." Our eyes remained locked as my muscles tensed.

"You've looked into him, right?" I raised an eyebrow, concerned with the idea of Hart seeing another man.

Tilting his head, Diggs responded with obvious sarcasm. "What do you think?" His tone shifted as he spoke. "I've looked into the guy, but haven't really found anything of importance."

Not good enough. "What's his name?" Diggs eyed me. "Do you at least know his address, where he works?" I tossed a small dirty rag over my shoulder. "Do you know if he has a record?" Diggs sighed, ignoring my questions. My patience wore thin as I glared at him showing that I was in no mood for his smartass attitude. "I want to know what you find out, because if he..." The threat died on my lips, my attention drawn away from Diggs by the sound of heels tapping down the stairs. *Saints save me.*

My eyes trailing up her toned legs squeezed into the tightest black leather pants that hugged her hips. She wore a thin, black mesh crop top that clung to her torso. My eyes couldn't help but stare as my blood boiled, my cock pushed against the zipper of my jeans at what she was wearing underneath—a knock-out pink bralette, obviously seen through the sheer fabric of her top, leaving little to the imagination. *Fuck, she looked delicious.*

"You'll what, V?" Diggs' voice forced *my* attention away from Hart. "Remember what we talked about. Let me worry about my sister. She is no longer any of your concern." *The hell she wasn't my concern.*

Hart reached the floor of the garage and grabbed a leather jacket, putting it on as she ran fingers through her dark, shoulder length hair. Her eyes met mine. "Close your mouth, V," she rolled her eyes, "you're drooling everywhere." Hart bumped my arm as she stepped past us. The smell of roses and blackberry filled the air, enticing me as she walked by, leaving without looking back. My eyes remained on her ass until she disappeared from my view.

I released a low, frustrated groan as my attention returned to Diggs. "Nothing, really? You have nothing to say about what she was wearing?" I placed my hands on my hips. "I mean, why even bother wearing clothes?" It wasn't the clothes that bothered me; it was the idea of her being with someone else. I struggled to contain my frustration, pulling my phone from my jeans pocket. My eyes stared at the dark screen, wishing it could tell me where she was going. Suddenly, my phone vibrated, blinking to life as a single text message came through.

Digg the Dick: 214 Lovedale Avenue.

My head snapped up, looking at Diggs as he held his phone and stared back at me."Don't get caught." I smirked, quickly grabbing my leather jacket. "V?" Diggs stopped me, "if you *do* happen to get caught, it wasn't me."

"Sure thing." I winked.

"How could she do this to us, MooMoo?" I looked at my sweet boy, his muzzle resting on my leg as we sat on a park bench. Milo released an audible huff as I placed my hand on his head and pet him gently. "I mean, honestly, you are the cutest, bestest boy, and, well," I glanced around the dark street, "I'm me. So this guy can't compare, right?" Milo licked my hand. "I knew you'd agree." I scooped my pomeranian up, showering his precious little face with kisses. "My little prince." With another huff, I carefully moved him back to the bench, his leash loosely in hand.

The sidewalk remained empty, giving me a clear view of the restaurant entrance, the same location Diggs sent me earlier— where Hart was having her 'date'. I fully intended to do as Diggs advised and not get caught. I was just curious and had this overwhelming need to keep her safe. I wasn't sure if it was my gut or what, but I didn't trust this guy. Not with her.

The sound of the front doors opening caught our attention as Hart and the mysterious man exited the restaurant. She seemed happy, smiling at the man as he looked down at her. Jealousy bubbled in my stomach as Milo growled, fully aware of my mood shift. "Shhh. Remember, she can't know we're watching her." The man hugged Hart goodnight, walking away as she pulled her phone from her leather pants. Milo quietly barked, recognizing his favorite woman. "Milo—" before I could quiet him, he jumped down from the bench, briefly looking back at me before bolting towards Hart, dragging his leash from my hand. "Milo!" I yelled after him, rushing behind, as his barks alerting Hart to our presence. *Fuck.*

"Milo?" Her eyes widened as she bent down to embrace the excited pomeranian. He jumped into her arms, licking her face as she smiled and giggled. Huffing, I slowed my pace as I approached them, her eyes moving to me as her grin faded. "What the hell are you doing here, V?" She stood, Milo tucked sweetly in her arms.

I stuffed my hands in my pockets, thinking of what to say. "Can't a man and his dog enjoy a late night stroll?"

Hart ignored my smirk, loving on Milo. "Uh-huh."

"So," I shifted my weight, "how was the date?" Hart's eyes glared at me.

"My dating life is no longer any of your concern." She carefully placed Milo on the ground, extending his leash out to me. "Try not to lose him again."

"Baby, I'm like glitter." I quickly moved towards her, our bodies inches away, "You might not see me, but I'm always there." My hand cupped hers as I grabbed the leash, winking as she stared up at me with her cognac eyes.

Hart ripped her hand from mine, shoving past. "Not me," she snapped.

A small laugh escaped my lips as I turned to look at her. "We'll see about that." I quickly followed Hart, scooping her legs as I tossed her over my shoulder, completely surprising her.

"What the hell, V?!" she shouted. "Put me down!" She punched my back as Milo barked, wagging his tail at her.

"Sorry, babe, no can do," I teased as she struggled beneath my grip. "Besides, someone has to see you home safely, right, Milo?" I glanced down at him as he danced beside me. "Now," I slapped Hart's ass, "let's get your momma home." Milo huffed in agreement.

HART

V carried me over his shoulder the entire way home. I wore myself out fighting his grip, eventually giving in, as it was pointless. My arm propped my head up as I stared down at Milo, prancing alongside his crazy dad. "I should've taken you with me when I left, huh, saved you from all this craziness." Milo barked at my words.

"Don't go putting crazy ideas in our son's head. Besides, you could've just stayed," V joked as we approached the steps of my home. It surprised me that he even remembered where I lived after all this time. He bent down, gently allowing me to step onto the sidewalk. As his face rose, our eyes met. V smiled, obviously content with himself, which only frustrated me more.

My arm swung as my palm landed harshly against his cheek. "*That's* for stalking me," I growled, "and *this*," I swung again as his hand caught my wrist mid swing.

V's face burned red from my impact as he smiled at me. "There are better ways to thank me, you know?" I'd had enough of his teasing as I yanked my arm from his grasp. I quickly turned, making my way to my door and unlocking it. As I entered my home, I turned to shut the door to see V leaning in the doorway, Milo in his arms. "Can I help you?" I snapped.

V patted Milo's head. "Just waiting for my goodnight kiss."

I scoffed, leaning down as I softly kissed Milo's head. "There. Goodnight."

"What about me?" V joked. I slammed the door in his face, quickly locking it. The sound of his muffled laughter seeped through the door. "We're wearing her down, Milo."

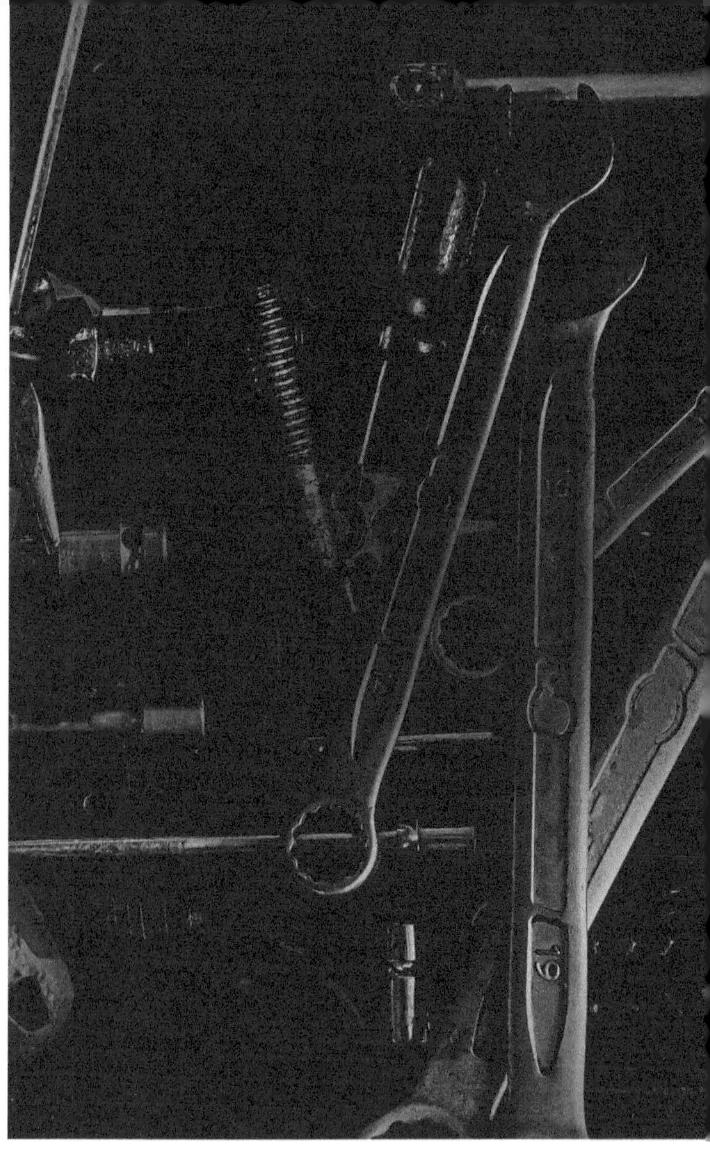

Chapter Four
THE SAINT'S FUNDRASER

V

Leaning against the workbench, my fingers scrolled through my phone, waiting for Diggs to finish up his call. His tone was flirty and low—must be on the phone with his latest boo thang. I was patiently waiting for the latest update on the Keepers. Hart huffed as she stormed into the shop. "Good morning, sunshine," I teased, "how'd you sleep?"

She stopped, glaring at me as she rolled her eyes. "Ugh!" Hart scoffed as she quickly stormed away.

"What did you do?" Diggs groaned, motioning toward Hart as the two of us made our way up to his office.

"*Technically* nothing." I joked, throwing my

hands up in defense.

"What do you mean *technically*? Damn it, V, this isn't going to come back on me now, is it?" We stepped into the Cathedral office as I cleared my throat.

"Hey, I didn't tell her *where* I got the address from… So you're good."

Diggs shook his head. "Let's hope so." Despite our differences, neither one of us wanted to be on Hart's bad side.

My body plopped down in a chair across from Diggs, lightly spinning as he watched me. "Well, if you're done chatting it up with your flavor of the week," I motioned to his phone, "Nicholas is expecting an update on the Keepers, as well as an update on any known movement from the other families."

"Rumor is the Lykos family are indeed preparing to make a move against the Saints," Diggs sighed, leaning back, "but our contacts aren't exactly talking." The mood of the room shifted.

"What do you think their motives are?" My chair halted as I leaned forward.

"All I can think of is that they discovered

what we were looking into, but the history between the two families goes way back, so there's really no telling. The Lykos family has always been one of the Saints' biggest threats."

"Do you know why? I know the rumors and stories behind the families, but is there any truth to it?" The history of the Saints and the Lykos family stretched far into the past, but not much was really known when it comes to the animosity between the two prominent organizations.

"I'm not sure, but I am reaching out to a few of my personal contacts. Everything happening with the Keepers and the Havens going quiet, it's best we prepare for anything and everything."

"Speaking of the Havens," I propped my elbows on my knees, "have you heard anything about the Kings yet? I'm beginning to get a little worried." *It's not like Angel to go silent.*

"We did hear that she arrived at the Kings, but nothing new since. Let me reach out to a friend in the area; he may be able to help us get in contact with her." I nodded in agreement.

The heaviness of the room lightened as Hart stepped into the office, grimacing at the sight of me. I couldn't help but smile as she approached Diggs. "Will I see the two of you tonight at the gallery for the Saints annual fundraiser?"

Hart scoffed as Diggs glanced up at her, one hand on her hip, the other leaning against the chair. "Those formal events aren't exactly our thing, right, Diggs?" Her brother forced a smile up at her. "Besides, I wouldn't want to upset your owner." I knew she was referring to Nicholas.

"Hart," Diggs snapped.

"What?" She crossed her arms visibly frustrated.

"Nicholas is our boss. We're just as much a part of the Saints as V," he motioned in my direction, "show some respect." I knew she disliked Nicholas due to our past, but I hadn't realized how deep her scars went.

She rolled her eyes. "Unlike others, some of us didn't choose this life."

"Nonetheless, we are a part of the Saints." She went quiet, obviously upset with the reality of their situation. Hart and Diggs had been a part of the Saints for years, almost as long as myself. How they ended up in this family was unknown, but it always made me wonder.

"Well," I broke the tension standing from my chair, "I got to be honest, I'm going to miss seeing you in a dress." I winked. Hart pulled her eyes away, her cheeks flushed as Diggs shook his head. "You too, Diggs."

"I'll show you my dress another time, Val." Diggs jokes. Hart smacked his arm as he laughed lightly to himself.

Chapter Five

THE PARTY

V

Soothing music filled my ears as an elegant string band played at the opposite end of the large open gallery. The various art pieces up for auction were on display against the stark white wall of the gallery. My gaze snagged on one piece in particular, admiring the detail of the work. Catching a waiter as they passed behind me carrying a tray of champagne, I said to myself, "Don't mind if I do."

I went to grab one glass before spotting Nicholas and Vixen reaching the top of the stairs. Smirking to myself when Nicholas stopped Vixen from removing her hand from where it rested on his forearm. *Possessive asshole.* "Better take a few," I winked at the waiter, carefully grabbing three glasses of the sparkly champagne. Extending my hand as they approached offering them a flute, Vixen gave me a soft smile of gratitude before taking the drink.

"Nice suit," Nicholas teased, pointing to my custom-made, bubblegum pink suit that had been paired with a heart-patterned bow tie. My hair was styled in a half up bun as opposed to my normal top knot. I beamed with pride before turning back to refocus on the piece of art in front of me.

"Gotta stand out somehow." I smiled. Nicholas was dressed in one of his usual formal, midnight black suits, his hair styled back and wearing his ever-present, gold stag ring.

"Be nice, Nicholas," Vixen smirked, her red lips darker than usual, giving his arm a gentle squeeze. She was wearing a form fitting, red lace dress with long sleeves—an obvious nod that she was *his*. Together, their presence reflected power and position. She raised the bubbling champagne to her lips, her green eyes glued to Nicholas, as he placed his hand on the small of her back.

"Me being nice ends with you," Nicholas smirked, pulling her close to him as he nestled close to her ear.

I shook my head. "You two are ridiculous." Nicholas shot me a quick glance, smirking, clearly pleased with himself before turning to kiss Vixen's cheek.

He took a sip of his champagne. "How's everything at the Cathedral?" His tone lowered. "Surprised the building's still standing." Nicholas lightly bumped my arm as he raised his brow, the real question hidden beneath his words. Reaching up, I adjusted my bow tie that now felt slightly tighter than before.

"Been playing Cupid lately?" Vixen teased with a smile.

"Too bad he can't find someone for himself." Her voice instantly pulled my attention away as I turned to see Hart standing on the other side of me. My breath caught, body frozen as I took her in, the noise of the room fading to the background. She stood tall, dressed in a silky pale pink, corseted, full length dress. Hart's usual bun was nowhere to be seen, choosing instead a classic hollywood curl that brushed the top of her shoulder just above a cursive inked tattoo. Struggling to pull my focus from her breast pulled tightly by the dress, I forced my gaze down her hourglass figure, which was on full display. A slit up the left side not leaving much to the imagination. My blood boiled as I nervously adjusted the jacket of my suit, consumed by the sight of Hart. She stepped closer, heels tapping as she shifted to my left side. As Diggs took up the space between Nicholas and Hart, the group formed a loose circle. "Aren't you going to introduce me?" Hart smiled, her glossy, nude-colored lips drawing my eyes.

A matching smile stretched across my face as I gestured to my right, "Nicholas you already know." With a subtle nod of recognition I motioned over to Vixen. "Alessandra, this is Hart—Hart, meet Alessandra, Nicholas's better half." Diggs cleared his throat, reminding me of his presence, "and her brother Diggs."

With my gaze on Diggs's, I catch the way his jaw tightens for just a moment before softening. Extending his hand first to Nicholas and then to Vixen, he said, "It's nice to finally meet you, Alessandra," with a small smile to Nicholas, who returned his hand on her lower back. Vixen accepted his hand, giving it a small shake. As Diggs released her hand, the tension that had faded for a moment returned.

"It's nice to meet you both." Vixen glances at the siblings before turning her attention to Hart. "I have heard a *lot* about you," she said, throwing a wink in my direction.

"All good things, I'm *sure*." Hart looked at me, raising a brow as the last of her words slowly left her luscious lips.

A waiter approached the five of us, offering a silver platter of elaborate chocolate tarts.

"Thank you." Diggs quickly grabbed a tarte topped with gold flakes and a chocolate stag imprinted coin. He took a bite as the waiter made his way around us, offering the tray of desserts. Retrieving one tarte, Hart held it out to me and proceeded to grab one for herself. Vixen reached out to take one as Diggs gently interrupted, "I don't think you want that," pointing towards the tray.

"I'm sorry?" she questioned with a puzzled look on her face.

He raised his half-eaten tarte. "There's peanuts inside."

Vixen quickly pulled her hand back as Hart looked from her to Diggs. "What's wrong with peanuts?"

"I'm allergic," Vixen responded, looking at Diggs. "Thank you." He nodded.

Nicholas' demeanor changed as he glared at the waiter. "Take them to the back. Now." He growled.

The waiter, obviously fearful, replied, "Yes, sir."

Reaching out, I took the champagne he still held now that this would need to be addressed. "Sorry to cut our visit short, but it seems we have something to handle." Nicholas placed Vixen's hand back on his forearm, nodding goodbye as the two headed toward the kitchen.

Diggs's phone rang, his ridiculous ringtone blaring as he quickly tried to silence it. "Sorry," he looked at the bright screen, "gotta take this." I couldn't help but smile and shake my head as he hurried away.

Realizing it was just the two of us, Hart quickly took a swig of her champagne, avoiding eye contact. I did the same, unsure of what to say.

"So," she broke the tension, "still a fan of pink I see." She pointed to my suit, amused by my choice.

"Like you forgot," I winked pointing to her dress. "It is my favorite color," panning my eyes slowly down her body and back up, "on you especially."

"Oh, Val," she scoffed.

I stepped closer. "I love the way your mouth moves when you say my name."

Hart extended her arm, gently pushing me back. "If I'm stuck here with you, then I'm going to need another drink."

"No one's forcing you to be here." My hand grabbed hers as it lay firmly pressed against my chest.

Hart yanked her hand back. "Diggs..." she sighed, "said I got to play my part." She went to grab a drink from a passing waiter.

"Let's go." Her head snapped back around to glare at me. As the waiter passed by Hart, she missed her chance to stop them.

"That's going to be a no." Her eyes met mine, the challenge clear. With that she turned to flag down another waiter. Stepping into her space I dropped my voice so only she could hear my next words. "It wasn't a request, *Sweetheart*."

HART

As we drove, passing streetlights cast slivers of light through the tinted windows of the car, briefly illuminating the darkness just long enough for me to steal glances at V while he stared out the front window. Trying not to draw his attention while admiring all of him, from the half up bun he wore, the golden locks pulled back to show his beautiful face, I couldn't see his soft warm eyes, knowing them as if they were my own, having lost myself in them so many times.

My eye caught on his luscious lips, his full bottom lip begging me to pull it between my teeth. He shifted, looking out the side window, which sent through me an overwhelming urge to run my tongue along his neck, gently scraping my teeth down the sensitive skin giving him the little bit of pain I know he enjoyed. Memories began rushing back to me as the warmth of the car magnified V's intoxicating scent. The mixture of his leather and musk clouded the air causing heat to pool low in my stomach. I bit my lip, *Why does he have to smell so good?* Shifting in the seat, I tried to subtly soothe the ache between my legs. When my eyes moved back up to his face, I was met with the reflection of a smirking V in the window. Rolling my eyes I turn my head forcing myself to look at anything else.

Coming to a stop outside the Cathedral, V paused before reaching for the door, removing his jacket. He slipped it around my shoulders before I could register what he was doing. Moving to open the door, I brushed my nose along the collar, taking in more of his alluring scent. Sliding across the seat toward the open door, I took his offered hand with a look, "Ever the gentleman." I smirk, placing my hand in his.

V paused, a look passing over his face before it cleared. "I have shown you I am no gentleman." With a wink, he guided me toward the side door. He turned to face me as he wrapped his arms around me.

"What are you doing?" I giggled, as he stared intently at me.

"I'm *waiting* for you to unlock the door," he pointed to the Cathedral. He was so close that his presence consumed my thoughts.

I extended my arms, motioning to my body. "And where is it that you expect me to keep a key?" I could feel his eyes as they traced every inch of my body. "Hey," I snapped my fingers towards his face. "Eyes up here, sir."

V smiled. "You're the one who made me look." I couldn't help but smile at his obvious flirting.

"Well," I sighed, my breath fogging in the cold air, "how are we going to get in?"

V pulled a set of keys out of his pocket, waving them around. "I guess it's a good thing Diggs gave me a key."

I shook my head as V turned to the door. "Yea, definitely a good idea to give you a key," I said sarcastically but knowing full well we'd be screwed right now if not for Diggs. Walking into the garage, I eyed his bike propped on its stand. He had been working so hard on it, replacing parts and doing general maintenance. I could tell when he brought it in that it hadn't been ridden in a while. My hand lightly brushed across the bike, feeling the two hearts pierced by an arrow stitched into the leather seat—*our symbol.* I could feel V's eyes heavy on me as I slowly removed his jacket and draped it over the handlebars of the motorcycle.

V

I watched as Hart propped herself against my motorcycle, placing her hands on either side of those delectable hips causing her breast to push against the fabric of her dress. I could tell she was trying to look anywhere but at me. *Oh Sweetheart, did you get your fill in the car?* I couldn't help but bite my lip at the sight of her. Shifting to move closer, I spotted something out of place in the dimly lit shop. A large vase of bright red roses sat on one of the workbenches. Turning I moved closer to inspect the flowers. Slipping the card from its holder, *Hart* was scribbled on one side. Tossing the card down I slipped one of the roses from the bouquet turning back to Hart, who now looked slightly guilty.

"So *this* is what it takes to get your attention," I twirled the stem between my fingers as I closed the distance between us. Taking the rose, I guided the silky petals down her arm, causing a trail of goosebumps to cover her skin. She shifted her weight between her feet, drawing my eyes to see that she was still wearing the strappy, gold high heels. *Those cannot be comfortable.*

I leaned forward, closing the distance between us as I placed the rose next to Hart on the seat of the motorcycle.

My mouth lingered gently outside her ear, my voice lowering to a whisper. "Why don't we get a little more comfortable?" Before she could respond, I dropped to one knee. My hand slowly shifted the silky pink skirt of her dress to expose her knee. The tips of my fingers grazed her skin, running down until I reached her right ankle. "Lift." Hart obeyed my command, raising her leg.

Removing the shoe, I gently rubbed the arch of her foot, squeezing my way back to her ankle. She let out a low moan that went straight to my hardening cock, pulling a faint matching groan from my lips. "Sweetheart, I need to take the other shoe off before you start making those sounds."

Looking down at me through her lashes she whispered, "Yes, sir."

I carefully placed her foot back on the ground, lifting her left foot, my fingers slowly undoing the straps as I took my time removing her shoe. I made sure to give her left foot the same attention as the right, gliding my hand up her leg, squeezing, gently working it up to her knee.

I took a moment, inhaling deeply before slowly standing, my gaze meeting Hart's. The heat in her eyes mirrored my own. I could tell she wanted this just as badly as I did, but I needed to hear her say the words out loud. Reaching up I brushed the back of my hand against her cheek, "Do you want me?" I wanted her to want me—*needed* her to want me. She reached up, turning my palm to press it to her cheek as she breathlessly released a single word, "Yes."

"You understand what is going to happen?" Hearing the seriousness in my tone, she paused before she spoke with conviction, "Yes." *Good girl.* There was something else that I needed from her. Not wanting to waste any more time, I asked, "What's your word?" I needed to check in with her before this went any further. "Sweetheart, you know that we won't move forward until I hear you say your word."

Heart's dark eyes stared down at me as she whispered, "Cupid."

"Do you still use the same colors as pacers?" I asked to make sure we were on the same page.

"Green to keep going, yellow to slow down, red or cupid to stop." I knew then that she was taking this as seriously as I was.

I leaned down, excited by her confirmation. "Remember," placing my arms on either side of her, gripping the seat of the motorcycle, "just say your word, and we stop." My face hovered in front of hers, her breathing increasing as she nodded.

Chapter Six

THE RELEASE

HART

Having him this close was what I craved but would never admit to him. Intoxicated by the way his hands moved over my body, my mind began to quiet as I slowly let go... I hadn't felt this way in a long time. *I missed this. I missed him.* I lowered my head to signal my submission and show my trust in him to take control of the situation. Releasing the seat, his right hand felt like a brand as it brushed against my exposed leg. His hand slowly made its way to my neck. *Yes please.* I gasped as his grip tightened, enjoying his touch as he applied the perfect amount of pressure, edging me closer to climax. My body was wound tight, and I took slow measured breaths through my nose.

He leaned in, rubbing his thumb across

my lower lip before brushing his mouth across mine, the kiss gentle. I *wanted* more. Snaking his left arm around my waist, he pulled me upright. My breasts pressed against his firm broad chest. As the kiss continued, I could feel that he was being considerate of me, but that wasn't who we were. V moved to pull away, not wanting this to end. I chased his lips, the kiss growing from sweet to scorching as his tongue teased my mouth asking for permission; my lips opened for him as our tongues danced. My hands reached up swiftly untying and gripping the bow tie tails; I gently pulled him towards me whispering, "Now the puppy has a leash." V reacted to my words exactly as I planned.

His hand released my neck, grabbing my right wrist, causing the silky bow tie to slide from my grasp. Without hesitation, he effortlessly spun me. Surprised by the sudden movement, I giggled before my head fell back against his chest. Leaning in he ran his nose along the side of my exposed neck until he reached my ear, whispering, "You're going to regret that," as he nipped my earlobe, moving me so my hands rested at my side. His voice turned into a low growl, "Don't move your hands." Warm hands skated along my skin as he reached my shoulders, briefly feeling their absence only to return a moment later. His fingers traced my shoulder blades, lifting the delicate straps of my dress. With a quick sharp tug he sliced the dainty strap with his pocket knife, repeating the movement on the other, leaving both ends to hang loosely down the front of my dress.

Showing no patience for unlacing the corset top, he carefully sliced through the strings, allowing it to fall, the crisp air causing my nipples to peak. V flicked the blade closed, placing it back in his pocket. He released a low growl of approval as his warmth traveled down my back, admiring his work as the now ruined dress was draped at my waist, only being held up by the snug material. I gasped as the fabric was suddenly yanked down my body to fall around my feet. V extended his right hand allowing me to take it and step out of my discarded dress.

His weighted gaze sparked a hot flush

to rise to my cheeks. He leaned in close, gripping my backside before giving my ass a swat. My body jolted in response, the impact of his hand stinging. A soft moan escaped my lips at the feel of his erection pressing against me. Instinctively I pushed back into him, reveling in the response he had to me. Moving his hands around my waist, they lingered a moment before turning me to face him. With my body now on full display just for *him*, his eyes ignited a fire deep within me. Our eyes connected as he slowly worked his shirt open. Drawing out the time between each button until he reached the last one, tossing it to the garage floor. *Ever the tease.* Now shirtless, V pulled me flush to himself, taking my lips in an aggressive kiss. My gaze followed him over to the nearby engine lift. Stopping to look at me with hunger-filled eyes, a smirk played across his lips. He grabbed some hoop straps and a sling off the tool cart and started to work them into a makeshift swing. I watched the muscles in his back as he flexed hooking everything into place. V had always been built, the time apart not lessening the impact seeing his naked torso had on me. I wanted to map every inch of his body with my tongue, explore the new ink that decorated his skin. Turning to face me once again, he pats the sling and says, "Come." The commanding words, in stark contrast to the humor of his expression. I bit my lip, slowly making my way to him as my hips moved seductively.

I came to stand in front of V. He still wore his shoes and dress pants. My eyes raked over his tattooed chest, noticing new pieces. The dark tattoos highlighted the curves of his chest and abs. Pulling my lower lip between my teeth, wetness now coated the inside of my thighs. At the sound of V clearing his throat, my eyes snapped to his. His pupils had blown wide with lust at my obvious appreciation of his glorious body. Without breaking our eye contact, he toed off his shoes, kicking them to the side, before reaching and unbuckling his belt. Leaving it loose as he stared down at me, he commanded, "Take it off." I undid his pants, giving them a tug they fell to the floor. Kicking them to the side, V stood looking like a tattooed god. Reaching out he placed one hand at the nape of my neck gently pulling me to him. My skin blazed as our bare chests met as V brought his mouth to mine in a bruising kiss. V broke away and said, "Tell me again. What's your word?" Drunk on the moment I uttered, "Cupid."

"That's *my girl*," he growled as he swept me up into his arms and sat me on the swing. Placing my foot into the strap, he whispered, "How many times do you think I can make you cum, *Sweetheart*?" Grinning at him, I sarcastically answered, "Probably not even one time." With mischief in his eyes he looked at me and said, "Bet."

V kneeled before mc as he slid his hand down my thigh, pausing over my recently acquired ink. "Don't think I didn't notice..." Leaning in he began to place gentle kisses down the inside of my right leg. Coming closer to my dripping wet center. Passing it by, he moved to the other leg, giving it the same attention until he reached my knee. I let out a frustrated groan, and his low chuckle caused my annoyance to spike. I rolled my hips trying to gain any amount of friction to soothe the ache that had been building at my center. V halted my movement with a quick pop of his hand on my needy cunt.

"Oh Fuck."

Running his finger through my folds, he smeared the wetness, grazing my clit before pulling back. Groaning again, I was met with another swift smack. Enjoying the sting I moved again, knowing what the consequence would be, but I didn't care—I wanted it. Needed it. With another slap, my climax rolled over me, just as V slid a finger inside me, setting off another release. "That's two already." *I am screwed or I will be.*

V

She was going to think twice about being a brat, knowing I aimed to please. Using pleasure as punishment, she wouldn't have another orgasm left in her once I finished. I pulled my finger from her, rubbing my thumb across her swollen nub. "You are so soaking wet, Sweetheart." Returning to her entrance, I slid two fingers in, coating them with her essence. She clenched around me, moaning as I thrust in and out. I continued until I felt her begin to move, her walls spasming with another release. A moan slipped past her lips as I pulled my fingers out. Her lids were heavy as she looked down her body. Meeting her gaze I slid the two coated fingers in my mouth. A throaty groan worked past my lips. "Mmm, sweet as sugar." Now that I had a taste, I needed more.

Above me, Hart shifted her hips letting out a whimper. *Greedy girl.* "Was three *not* enough?"

Without missing a beat, her words came as almost a whisper, "Stamina does drop for old men..."

Old man? I give her a feral grin. "Remember that when you can't stand later." With that, I dove in, running my tongue up her dripping center. Taking her clit between my teeth, I bit down gently, a sharp cry coming from above me. Releasing the abused nub from my bite, soothing it with long licks, I said, "I think it's time for another." Slipping two fingers back inside her, I found her sweet spot. Alternating sucking and rubbing her clit until she was right on the edge. She released a sigh of frustration as I removed my mouth from her, slowing my fingers as her building climax faded slightly. Right as she began to move, I started again, slower than before. I began to torture her again with long slow strokes of my tongue, bringing her right to the edge. When I nipped her clit again, she started to climax. I pushed three fingers inside her, using her release to drive my fingers deep inside. Hart came with a silent scream. Her walls pulsing around my fingers as I continued to thrust in and out until she slumped back, spent.

Kissing the inside of her thigh, I rose, standing between her spread legs as I looked down at her. "Sweetheart." Placing my hand against her cheek, I leaned in, her eyelids fluttering open. Giving her a moment, I needed to check in with her. "Are you with me?"

As her eyes cleared and met mine, she softly responded, "Yes."

"I need your color." My thumb slowly

stroked across her cheek.

"Green."

Giving her a slow smile, I brought my mouth down to her lips. Teasing her mouth open, I deepened the kiss. I snaked one hand between us as she wrapped her warm hand around my cock. I was hard as steel as she rubbed my head against her folds. One push and I would be inside her.

"Please, Sweets." With that, she notched me at her opening as I looked into her beautiful cognac eyes. Despite her wetness, it was a pleasingly tight fit.

Pulling out to the tip, I set a leisurely pace. Letting us both come back from the edge. When I knew I could continue without blowing early, I started again. When I changed the depth of my thrust, Hart squeezed the head of my dick with her walls. *Fuck.*

Thrusting myself to the hilt, we both let out matching groans, and I set a bruising pace. Wrapping my hands around her hips, I swung her toward me, slamming her against me. My eyes roamed over Hart—she was stunning. Her eyes were closed in pleasure. Little drops of sweat dotted her brow and chest. Her skin glistened under the lowlights of the shop. I needed her to come. Slipping my arms under her back, I lifted her body from the swing. This new position brought me as deep as possible. As I gripped her ass in my hands, she wrapped her legs around my waist. "God, Sweetheart, I could live inside you." Pumping up into her, I turned us, walking towards a random car. *Apologies to the owner.*

Hart hissed when her back came into contact with the cool metal of the car. I silenced her with a rough kiss. Nipping her lip before deepening this kiss. Pulling us away from the side of the car, I lifted her off my cock, letting her feet come to rest on the cold concrete floor. Turning around to face the car, Hart's words came low and excited. "Um, this is a customer's car."

"Yes, it is, so let's not get it too dirty." My reply came out low and full of humor. Finding the handle, I pulled the door open crowding her closer to the open backseat. Sliding my hand up her back, her skin pebbled with goosebumps. I pressed my palm between her shoulder blades to signal for her to bend over. Before she could react, I thrust inside her, choosing a punishing speed.

"I want to hear you one more time, baby," I gritted through clenched teeth. "Nothing will bring me more pleasure than your sweet pussy milking me dry." Pounding my cock inside her, I could feel my climax barreling toward me. "Come. Now!" I commanded, slipping my hand forward to tweak her nipple, pinching it between my thumb and forefinger. At the slight tug, Hart clamped down on me.

"Valentine... Fuck yes... Right there." With a final thrust, Hart began to quiver as her climax overtook her. Fucking her thoroughly, I let go. My hot cum painted her insides.

Laying on the back seat, we caught our breath. I kissed the top of Hart's head, leaning away to ask, "How was that for an old man?"

"Meh, it was ok," Hart teased.

Chapter Seven

THE WAKE-UP CALL

V

I slowly woke to something lightly tickling my face. With a puff of air, I made a mental note to book Milo for a grooming. Talking quietly in the voice saved for the sweetest boy, "Moo Moo, we talked about this you can't—" I froze, my brain registering that it was not Milo's hair on me…but Hart's. *My Sweetheart.* Last night couldn't have gone better if I had planned it. Waking this morning to her warm, naked body entangled with mine was icing on the cake. Brushing the hair back from her face, I studied the beautiful lines of her features. This was the time I truly missed having with her. Memories rushed in of slow lazy mornings with her and Milo hogging the bed. We would usher Milo out of the room for his breakfast, because no son should witness what their parents get up to. Getting him settled allowed us time to get lost in each other. Taking control in the bed allowed Hart to let go. That was what happened last night. She let me past the wall—the wall she built around herself. I kissed her temple and let my eyes fall closed. Her soft breathing lulled me back to sleep. *Please don't lock me out again.*

Hart

Tap, tap, tap.
What the hell is that noise?
Tap, tap, tap. The sound loudened, pulling me from sleep. That was the best sleep I had gotten in ages. Moving to roll out of bed, my hand met warm, bare skin as memories of the previous night came rushing back. Being at the gallery, leaving with V, coming back to the Cathedral, being able to let go... I didn't trust anyone to see me like that...except *him.*

"Listen, we have got to open the shop, and you two being, well, like this," he pointed, "is kind of preventing that."

The sound of my brother's voice was like

a bucket of cold water being poured over my head. I shot upright, startling my sleeping companion. V's eyes flew open, in a surprising move as he yanked me down rolling to cover my very naked body. *Shit. Fucking shit.*

"V, I want to see your naked ass about as much as I want to see my sister's." Diggs's voice was muffled by the glass of the windows. Peering out from under V, I caught my brother's eye before he turned his back to us. "I doubt the dress Hart had on last night is in one piece?" With a thud, a pair of coveralls landed on the roof of the car, followed by V's pants. With that, Diggs stepped away from the car allowing us a moment.

"Well...that was—" my words were caught as I took in V's expression. His eyes darted around like he was looking for a threat. Reaching up, I gently placed my hand on his cheek, turning his face towards me, whispering a nickname that has not passed my lips since I left: "*Sweets.*" V's eyes cleared, his mask sliding back into place.

"This is going to be a fun little chat." With a quick peck to my lips, V unfolded his massive form from the car. As he stood outside the door, I was met with a view of the most gorgeous ass. *God, I wanted to sink my teeth into it.*

Tossing the coveralls inside to me, he shut the door before pulling his pants on. I dreaded pulling the coveralls on without anything underneath. With limited options, it was either a little uncomfortable or nude. Once dressed, I glanced around trying to spot where V and my brother had moved to. Pieces of their conversation drifted into the car. While it wasn't completely clear, I could understand them.

V

Stepping to the back of the car, Diggs was propped against the trunk scrolling through his phone. While I didn't want to talk to the older brother of the woman I just fucked, I knew it had to be done.

"So, I see our little talk had its usual effect on you?" Diggs questioned without shifting his attention from his phone.

"Listen—" I started in a hushed tone when Diggs' eyes snapped to mine, the words dying in my throat.

Slipping his phone in his pocket, he sharply retorted back. "No, V, you listen. I try to not mess around in Hart's life. She's a grown woman who makes her own choices," he glanced up and down my still half naked body, "even if they are poor choices." *Kick me in the balls next time, why don't you?* His eyes bore into mine. "Don't make her time your last priority."

I felt like I had just been sucker punched in the gut, the air rushing from my lungs. I was left trying to force air past the massive lump in my throat.

I quickly changed the subject by asking an equally important question. "Anything on Angel?"

Diggs let out a heavy sigh. "No, it's not Angel I'm worried about."

"The fuck you better—" My anger came boiling to the surface.

"Calm down, what I was saying is she is not the one I am concerned about.

She is tough as hell and could take care-of herself in any situation." Wiping his hand down his face, Diggs covered his eyes for a brief moment. Movement caught my attention over his shoulder. Hart was dressed and trying to squeeze out of the car. Feeling my gaze on her, she cut her eyes in my direction. With a subtle shake of my head to tell her to stay put. I knew Diggs wanted her kept out of this, but it was more dangerous for her to be kept in the dark.

"I heard back from one of my contacts, and Nicholas is not going to be excited by what I've learned. There are some connections to Lykos family that we weren't aware of. It seems Deyanira has been moving people, and that someone important to the family had to be pulled back after getting pretty roughed up. Apparently, he almost died." Diggs finished, giving me a moment to process as he nervously spun the ring on his hand. This was something he had always done. The silver-plated ring was the only piece of jewelry I had ever seen Diggs wear. It was an outward sign of his place within the Saints.

The Keepers, one of the many inner circles of the Saints. I stared at the gold signet ring, the wings of the engraved angels catching the light. The small black onyx gemstone sparking with each turn. Angel also had a bad habit of spinning her ring when she was nervous, not that I would ever call her on it.

"Cut the cryptic bullshit, Diggs. What 'fucking connections' and who's the person?" My patience had worn thin from his secrecy. Before Diggs could reply, my phone rang, the screen showing Milo's sitter. *Shit, my poor sweet boy.*

"I have to go, but we aren't done here." I glared in Diggs direction. Answering the phone, I turned to leave as I was met with a very upset pup on the other line. "Moo Moo, I am so sorry. I promise I did not forget about my boy." I tried to use my most soothing tone. "I am on my way home now, Milo Moo. Who's the bestest bo—" My words were cut off by someone coming in, and I started to apologize for almost bumping into the guy. "Good dog." He smirked. *I'm going to kill him.*

Standing directly in my path was the dick

head Hart was supposedly dating. Walking past me and into the shop as if he owned the place, he walked straight to where Diggs, and now Hart, stood.

"Shit, I completely forgot. Give me five minutes and then we can stop by my place so I can grab some clothes."

What. The. Fuck.

Chapter Eight

THE CLAIM

HART

Working on a particular customer's car, I couldn't help but to let my mind wonder what happened the other night with V, making it harder to be in a relationship. Music blared through my earbuds as I remembered the feel of him inside me and the many ways he made me cum. Trying to reach further into the hood, I got on my tiptoes. A moment later I felt something press into my backside, pinning me against the hood of the car. "What the fu—" I turned to look but I was held firmly in place. Removing one of my earbuds, V leaned in growling, "Did you forget?"

"What are you doing?" I say in a hushed tone only loud enough for him to hear. "Everyone will see—"

"Did you forget?" he repeated gruffly,

wrapping my hair around his fist.

"Forget what, Valentine?" I spat back. All I'd done was think about him since last night and what we did.

"You are mine. Every moan, every scream, and every orgasm… It's all *MINE*."

Leaning harder into me, his hands begin to trail down my body. "V, we can't do this here. The others—" I tried to say as he grabbed the inside of my thigh with a bruising grip, causing me to release a sigh of pleasure.

"What was that?" he whispered into my ear as his hand slipped further towards my center. Just the feel of him against me had me dripping wet. My fist clenched around the tool I was holding when his fingers reached the band of my panties tracing along it. *Fucking tease.* "Do you want a little reminder?" he asked, nipping my earlobe before moving to kiss my neck. When one of his fingers ran through my drenched folds, my control began to fray. *Yes, yes, yes,* becoming a mantra in my head. Stroking his finger over my sensitive nub had me on the edge of release. I spoke the word without meaning to, "Yes." Slipping a finger in, he rubbed over my g-spot and whispered, "So close, Sweetheart." His words were low and seductive as he continued to draw me closer to orgasm. Right as my muscles began to tense, V pulled his hand out of my coveralls. His lips brushed over my ear, "Does he get you this wet? Does this greedy pussy drip for him?" He turned and walked away, leaving me clenching around nothing and wanting everything. Ripping the other earbud out, I was met with silence and an empty shop.

"What the fuck, Valentine?" I yelled at V's retreating form. Throwing his hand up in a wave, he pushed through the door and was gone.

Chapter Nine

THE RIDE

V

Carefully opening the shop door, I expected Hart to be waiting, tool in hand to lob at my head. Had it been a dick move to come in and tease her? Yes. Did I feel like she earned a little teasing? Also, yes. But damn, it was torture watching her leave with that asshat, especially after the night we had. Could I have been better in the past about being more attentive to her needs? Yes, but did I have much of a choice? No. I could have said something to Nicholas about all the late nights and being pulled away; he would have understood, but it was harder because of everything the Saints had done for me. Hart didn't know all of the details of what it was I'd been doing with the Saints and the lives I had been a part of saving. I couldn't say that I regretted it. I was able to be a part of something much bigger than me and in some way repay the Saints in a way. I ran my fingers through my hair to break apart the braid. I had no shame in admitting that I was particular about my hair. I kept multiple hair ties with me just in case. Hart was the person that spurred this trait. After a long motorcycle ride, my hair would be a rat's nest, and Hart took to braiding the part that was exposed. When things ended with her, I stopped riding but learned to do that for myself, and it had come in handy over the years.

Surveying the shop, I listened for signs of Hart. I knew she was here—she always got to the shop before everyone else. I noticed the light upstairs was on. *Must not have had her coffee yet... That's terrifying.* Making my way quietly up the stairs, I stepped through the folding glass wall with one side collapsed inward to make a doorway into the *Keepers* meeting room. To anyone else who came up here when it was closed, it would look like just a wall of windows, but in reality, it was mirrored, bulletproof glass that made the upstairs of the Cathedral a stronghold. I was met with the smell of coffee and soft humming. Leaning against the doorway of the breakroom, I watched Hart in the kitchen area. The room was not used by the employees of the shop and was more for the Keepers and the Hart siblings. Meetings were held here, but Keepers would use the upstairs to unwind when they were moving their charges. For a lot of the people we helped, this was the first stop they made. While it wasn't a luxury hotel, it had all the basic necessities covered. Some comforts were added to this room, like the full bar, an oversized couch, and massive TV. The kitchen area had basic appliances, but Hart required caffeine, so a stocked coffee bar had been added. Diggs on the other hand had added multiple gaming systems. *Nerd.* Not that I would say that to him, because I gamed with him and he would call me on my bullshit.

It took Hart a moment to realize she was no longer alone. Turning she pulled one of the earbuds out scowling before turning back to her coffee. "Fuck off."

With a snicker I walked in. "Well, good morning, sunshine. I see we have not had our coffee yet." She cut her eyes at me for a moment before rolling them and returning to her coffee.

"If you think coffee will improve my mood around you, you would be sadly mistaken." Grabbing her cup she pushed past me, moving to the doorway and throwing her hand up in a wave like I had done to her the day before.

"Still salty I see," I called with a laugh, following behind her as she made her way to the shop floor. When she got to the bottom of the stairs, instead of going to her bench, she turned toward the stereo system. *Oooh, she is going to drown me out, fat chance.* I moved in behind her, bracketing her body between my arms. My chest barely brushed her back as she sucked in a surprised breath. Leaning forward I pressed my now hardening cock to her lower back. My mouth hovered next to her ear, "You used to enjoy a little delayed gratification." Lowering my head to nip the side of her neck before soothing the skin with a kiss. "You know how much pleasure can come when you have a little patience." My words ghosted across her skin causing her body to give a small shiver. I placed another kiss on her neck as she grinded her ass against my solid length. I pulled back before giving her a swat on her ass. "Now get that luscious peach of an ass outside and on my bike. While you won't be riding me, yet my bike will work for now."

Hart

No longer feeling V behind me, I turned to see him waiting for me to follow. *Damn.* I knew what he was doing. This was how he has always played, and I fucking missed it. I haven't trusted anyone with my more vulnerable side. He draws out my pleasure, controls when and how many times I climax, getting his gratification from pleasing me. While most people would love endless orgasmic bliss, me included, there was an openness between us during aftercare. We were able to connect on a deeper level. An idea sparks for this little motorcycle trip. Grabbing my keychain with my wallet and keys, I slid my phone in my pocket. *You want to play, Sweets? We'll play.*

V was propped up on his motorcycle, looking through a backpack. When the door closed, he looked up, smirking around the valentine sucker in his mouth. "Alright, Sugar, since you don't know where we're going, you have to hold on to supplies." Walking over I popped the sucker from his mouth and deposited it into mine. Taking the backpack from his hand, I pulled the sucker from my mouth, flattening my tongue to lick the sweet candy. "Mmm, cherry. My favorite."

V's eyes snapped to where I toyed with the sucker, causing him to pull his bottom lip between his teeth. Not giving him a chance to reply, I noticed the spare helmet on the seat. I leaned in, placing my hand on his hip, the warmth of his skin burning through his shirt. *This ride was going to be so fun.*

"Excuse me, safety first." With a slow exhale V stepped away to allow me to snag the helmet to put on. With my most innocent smile, I looked at him and asked, "Ready?

"Yeah...Yep...Yes, climb on."

Getting flustered so soon?

Climbing on I straddled the bike, getting comfortable in the seat before V climbed on. Before he pulled his helmet on, I knew what he was going to ask. Reaching my hand out, I was rewarded with a soft smile as he passed the elastic to me. I ran my fingers through his beautiful golden locks, relishing in how soft they were. V loved to have his hair played with, and I think it was one reason he kept it longer. Dividing the hair into three sections, I did a simple braid. Just something to keep his hair from tangling while we rode. Pressing my chest to his back and wrapping my arms around his waist, I gave him a gentle squeeze, signaling that I was ready.

Weaving between cars as we made our way out of town, traffic began to thin, allowing me to have a little fun. Relaxing my grip, I slipped my hand down closer to V's lap. Resting my palms on his muscled thighs, I gently rubbed up and down the tops of them. The road flattened out, allowing V to slide one hand down to take one of mine. He twined our fingers together, loosely holding my hand. I craved the warmth his body gave off. While it wasn't cold, the wind was chilly as we rode toward the mountain. Coming to an intersection, my heart melted when V stopped and flipped up his visor, bringing the back of my hand to his lips. My skin heated at the sweetness of the gesture. V portrayed himself as the tough tattooed guy that did questionable things, but for me, he was soft, caring, and romantic.

Flipping his visor back into place, he pulled away from the intersection, turning us left heading towards the mountains and a beautiful lake. Knowing V would need both hands to drive, I could go back to my teasing. I placed my hand back on his thigh where it rested, so that he could use both hands to maneuver the now winding road. I moved one hand, gently brushing it over the crotch of his pants, trying to pass it off as an accident. I didn't linger but instead moved away, waiting for just the right moment to rub against him again. This time he would know it was purposeful. Shifting my right hand, I brought it to rest directly over his now hardening cock. *That's it, baby.* If we were going to *our* spot, then I had a little time left before we arrived. V's dick gave a little jump, prompting me to squeeze it ever so lightly, causing another jolt of movement. As I kneaded his impressive length, he grew more aroused under my touch. His cock strained against his zipper. I knew I was going to pay for this, but it would be worth it. Normally being a brat was not a goal, but today it was my sole mission.

The pull-offs and side roads at the start of the mountain were always the most crowded. The same went for the ones at the lake. No one was willing to drive farther into the mountains to get to the areas with less congestion. We had found our spot by mistake one weekend, making it a getaway away from everyday life. It was on a well-maintained stretch of road that was paved but still not traveled often. Most people didn't realize that the road ended within spitting distance of a lake. The area was never crowded, and in all the times we had ventured this way we had not seen anyone there. Before we turned off, I slowly began to rub, grinding my palm slightly on his cock. Teasing the pressure until he was twitching to only back off. I repeated the cycle while adding a squeeze until I knew he was ready to either kill me or fuck me senseless. I hoped for the latter after the little act he put on the day before at the shop. Giving him one more squeeze, we came to a halt at the lake. Within seconds the kickstand was down and V was ripping off his helmet, hanging it from the handlebar by the straps. Removing my helmet and placing it between my legs on the seat as I looked off in the distance, I ran my fingers through my hair trying to work out the tangles. V quickly snatched the helmet, placing it next to his. "No need to fuss over that right now."

Turning he grabbed my face between his hands, pulling me in for a rough kiss. Teasing the seam of my lips with his tongue. *I need to get off this bike, so I can climb him like a tree.* Shifting so my upper body was turned letting out a squeal when V hooked his arms beneath my armpits, lifting me like I weighed nothing. My legs wrapped around his waist, locking my ankles behind his back. His left hand grabbed the strap on the top of the bag, removing it to set on the ground.

Pulling his head slightly away, he gave me a teasing look, "If I didn't know any better, I would say you were trying to get me worked up, Sweetheart." His words came out breathy. I unlocked my ankles from behind, letting them come to rest on the ground. That kiss had my panties absolutely drenched.

Knowing I wanted to push him a little farther, I looked at him from under my lashes, trying for a sweet and innocent tone, "It was just so chilly on the ride up, I didn't want you getting cold." He gripped my chin, so I was forced to look at him. His hair was wild where it had come out of his braid. Loose strands blew across his face in the breeze. His pupils were blown wide, the black centers almost completely eclipsing the normal blue shade.

"I know somewhere it will be toasty warm," his voice coming out as a hoarse growl. "It's time to see what else that mouth can do." Leaning in, his words whispered across my lips, before he took my mouth, owning it and driving his tongue between my lips, exploring every inch of my mouth. My body submitted to the demand of his kiss.

"Do you trust me?" he asked, seriousness bleeding into his tone.

I thought for a moment, digging deeper down to find the answer. I had never stopped trusting him. While we had our issues, he never did anything to make me question the trust I put in him. Looking into his eyes, I gave him my honest answer.

"Yes, I do." *I never stopped.*

"Colors?" he asked in a clipped tone.

"Green, keep going, Yellow is slow, Red or Cupid we stop." As I finished the sentence, I dropped to my knees in front of him. Reaching my finger up I began to slowly undo the buckle of his belt. "My nonverbals are three taps on your thigh to stop." Letting my hand trail down to tap the place we always used.

With his belt open, I moved my hands back up to undo his jeans. Pulling the zipper down, the only barrier between me and his long thick length was the sheer material of his briefs. Rising up slightly, I chose to tease him a little longer. Pressing in closer, I ran my tongue up his covered length, placing a kiss on the tip that poked out of the top.

"Fucking shit, Sweetheart." His words came out as a low moan.

Blinking up at him, I said with mock concern in my voice, "I think he may be getting cold." With one hand I tugged the front of his briefs down, tucking the waistband behind his balls. If someone did happen to come back here, their view would be limited to V's back. While he didn't mind showing off, I was territorial. His cock sprang forward, hard as steel and ready for whatever I had planned. Gripping the base in my free hand, I slowly stroked up to the tip where a bead of precum was collected. Leaning in I pulled his head to my mouth, swirling my tongue around it like I had the sucker. I moaned at the taste of him on my tongue. V had kept his hands to himself until this moment, but that one moan flipped the switch. *About fucking time.*

V

"You have had your fun, now it's my turn." Reaching up I pulled the hair tie from my braid. Gathering her hair in my hands and tying it back from her face, I asked with a wicked smirk down at her, "You ready?" Without another word, I grabbed a hold of her hair, wrapping it around my fist, and started pumping in and out of her mouth. She reached up and held onto the base of my length, grounding herself to me. "That's it, baby! Take my dick like a good girl." As I pulled her hair tighter, Hart let out a moan around my dick letting me know she approved, and I picked up my pace. I admired the sight of her plump lips wrapped around my cock. *God, she's beautiful,* I thought, the sight sending me over the edge. "Fuck! Swallow it, *Sweetheart.*" I took my thumb and wiped away the leakage from the side of her mouth as I removed my cock. Placing the now coated digit on her awaiting tongue, I smirked and said, "You missed some." She flicked her tongue over it and smiled up at me. *She will be the death of me.*

Removing my thumb from her mouth, I offered my hand to help her stand, pulling the hair tie out to run my fingers through her hair, tangling them in her now loose strands. I took her mouth in a slow sweet kiss.

"Come on, Sugar," I said, giving her hand a little tug. Carrying the backpack on one shoulder, I led Hart towards the lake, the sun reflecting off the water. Setting the bag down I released Hart's hand to pull the supplies from the bag.

"What's all this? If I didn't know any better, I would think you are trying to woo me," she teased, the humor evident in her tone. Laying down the small blanket, I began to set out the small snacks that were in the bag.

"I never knew all it would take was adult lunchables to woo you." My words came out with a little laugh. "Have a seat, we can enjoy a little snack and then head back." A look crossed Hart's face at my mention of heading back. It looked almost like disappointment. *No need to be disappointed, Sweetheart, I'm not done yet.*

We sat in comfortable silence, munching on food and watching the water ripple in the breeze. Resting back on her hands, she let her head fall back and her eyelids close. I took this time to take her in. She had always been absolutely stunning. Her long dark lashes kissed the top of her cheeks. Her pouty pink lips begged to be kissed. I could spend every minute of my day admiring her. She rarely ever wore makeup, especially at the shop; this allowed the freckles that dotted her nose to be visible. The warmth of the sun caused her bare face to pinken slightly.

Not moving from her position, she let me know that I had been caught, "I can feel you ogling me." The corner of her lip pulled into a smile.

"Just planning how I am going to enjoy my dessert." My body heated as blood rushed south, my cock plumping.

Opening her eyes, she rolled her head to the side meeting my gaze. "Dessert? What dessert?"

Leaning into her space I brushed my lips across hers. "It's a special sweet treat that happens to be my favorite." My words came out in a whisper. With that I stood, extending my hand to her again. Reaching out, she gently placed her hand in mine, allowing me to haul her to her feet. Quickly collecting the items from our picnic, I shoved them into my backpack, my control slipping by the second.

Flinging the bag over my shoulder, we swiftly made our way back to the bike, where she went to grab her helmet from the handlebars. I wanted to find a fallen tree, bend her over it, sink my length into her warm channel and pull every orgasm I could from her. *She's probably dripping from that blowjob by the bike.* Needing to find out for myself, I dropped the bag, grabbing Hart's waist pulling her back against my chest. "Are you dripping for me?" Sliding my hand down the front of her pants, I reached her soaking wet pussy.

Her breathing hitched. "Fuuuuuck, you are so wet for me." My words tumbled out in a growl. As I glided my finger through her slick folds, Hart let out a small whimper as my middle finger dipped inside her. Slowly I thrusted the digit in and out. Pressing the palm of my hand against her clit, she began to grind down, seeking friction and release. "Such a bad girl. Are you trying to get us caught?" I finished the question as my tongue ran over the shell of her ear. "You need me to fuck you so badly that you will risk getting caught."

Growing more frenzied in her move-ments, she rolled her hips. "Please, I need it," she whimpered.

"It? You know that you have to tell me exactly what you need, baby." I continued to tease her. "Now, tell me, Sweetheart. What do you need?"

"I need to cum. Please," her voice low as she begged.

"How should I make you cum? Should I keep grinding my palm against your needy clit?" To emphasize my point, I ground my palm harder, pulling a stifled moan from her mouth. "Or should I bend you over right here and fuck you until you can't stand and beg me to stop?" She clenched around my finger, squeezing her walls.

"Oh, you would like that, huh?" Thrusting my fingers in a few more times before pulling them from her, I rested my other hand between her shoulder blades, "Grab the handlebars and don't let go." Following my command, her knuckles turned white with the force of her grip. Undoing her pants, I worked them down her legs until her perfect ass was at eye level. Reaching with both hands, I spread her, swiping my tongue over her glistening entrance.

"So sweet." Leaving no time for her to react, I dove in, licking and sucking as I slipped one hand over, driving two fingers inside, coating them in her essence. Pulling them out only to push my tongue inside.

Her head fell forward as I continued. "I'm close," she whispered. With that I moved them to circle her swollen nub, needing her to finish. My fingers returned to her entrance, pushing inside as I ramped up my speed. "Oh God, V," her moans turning into cries, "fuck, fuck, Sweets. Right there." With two more pumps of my fingers, Hart was shattering around me. I could feel her walls pulsing, my dick jealous it wasn't him. *Calm down, boy, you'll get your turn.* Pulling out, I placed a kiss on her perky cheek before helping her pull her pants back up. I tried to support her as she stood, flexing her hands to get blood flow back after gripping the handles so tightly. "I think we should take this home, so I can have a second helping of dessert," I said, giving her ass a swat before turning to grab the bag. When I turned back to the bike, I let Hart climb on and secure her helmet, before passing her the bag. Reaching forward she pulled my helmet off, extending her hand in offering. When I grabbed the helmet, she didn't release it. Instead, she gave it a little tug, getting my attention.

"You're not the only one that wants dessert, Sweets." Her words were laced with arousal.

Holy shit.

Chapter Ten

THE WAIT

HART

I started to rouse from the best sleep I had had in a while, the sun peeking through the window. I went to roll over when a strong arm held me firmly in place. "Where do you think you're going?" I smile, wiggling my ass back into his dick, feeling it twitch with excitement as I replied, "Nowhere, just snuggling in closer." I miss this. The warmth of his body seeping into mine, warming me to my core. Turning over so our chests pressed together, I stretched to place a kiss on V's jaw. With my lips pressed to his skin, my words were a low whisper, "Did you think I was trying to sneak away?" He brought his hand up brushing a stray hair away from my face, then grazed my bottom lip with his thumb as he said, "Baby, you're not going to be the one that got away." A shuddering breath left me as I leaned in, brushing my lips against his in a slow gentle kiss. A short and pointed huff had us breaking away. Turning to look over my shoulder, I was greeted by sweet Milo.

With one final disgruntled huff, Milo climbed his doggy stairs, coming to sit at the end of the bed. Untangling myself from V, I sat up and scooped the sassy Pomeranian up in my arms. "Is someone a little jealous?" I asked, baby talking to him as I kissed his handsome face. "He's really missed his mom. Huh, Moo?" He huffed again as if in agreement. *I've missed you too, little man.* V added nervously, "And he's not the only one…"

I kissed the top of Milo's head before turning to set him on the floor.

"Will you be a good boy for mommy and go lay on the couch?" I asked, still talking in the sweet tone reserved only for him. Being the sweetest boy, he walked out the door of the bedroom. Rolling my body back toward V, I started to kiss him, "Now, where were we?" The kiss started out tame but quickly escalated. "I think we were right about here." Sliding one hand between us, I fisted V's morning wood. Hissing at the contact, he began thrusting his hips.

"How fast do you think I can make you come, Sweets?" I asked, giving his shaft a gentle squeeze.

Releasing a shuddering breath, his words came out on a groan, "You keep doing that—not long."

Stroking to the tip, I twisted my wrist just enough to pull a low "Fuck" from V. I stroked back down before the shrill sound of my alarm began to sound.

"If you touch that phone, I swear, Sweetheart……" The heat in his blown pupils caused me to almost ignore the alarm. *Fuck, I can't be late to the shop.*

Giving him a quick peck, I released his straining erection and quickly got out of bed. "Sorry, Sweets, we have a client coming to pick up this morning and I need to double check everything."

Groaning dramatically, V flopped back on the bed rubbing his face. "Can we shower at least?"

"Why, when we are just going to come back and get dirty? Also, no we don't have time." With a wink, I went to start coffee. *I'll gladly pay for that later.*

Chapter Eleven
THE MUTT

V

Pulling up to the Cathedral, my dick was still rock hard against my zipper. Having Hart pressed against my back the whole ride, "accidentally" grazing her hand over my crotch, was the icing on a very frustrating cake. Parking the bike and removing my helmet, I grabbed her hand, pulling it from where it rested on my thigh. Once dismounted, I rounded on her, watching her expression go from mock innocence to heated with desire. "You know I don't forget when you have been a brat. That's two times, just this morning."

Before she could give a reply that would have gotten her in even more trouble, Diggs burst through the door. His eyes landed on us, and with quick steps he approached. *Oh shit, he might actually hit me this time.*

"Where the hell have you been? I have

been calling you for a fucking hour, Valentine." Snatching his phone from his pocket, he rapidly tapped the screen.

Hart glanced at me in question. She would never forgive me for keeping things from her again. "Listen, there are—" My phone began to sound, the ringtone alerting me that it was Nicholas. I watched as Hart's expression turned from unguarded to her walls going up with lighting speed. Answering the call, my eyes remained locked on her now cold and steely glare.

"Nicholas is every—" He cut me off.

"We have an informant from Lykos." His voice carried through the line. I knew Hart could hear him, and, dammit, for her sake I wasn't changing that.

"What's the plan to get them?" My heart rate began to pick up. If we planned to make a move on Lykos we needed this person alive and well.

"Diggs knows the details and can fill you in on the way here. Time isn't on our side, so hurry the fuck up."

With that the line went dead.

"I'm going to get what I need and the car." Diggs jogged across the parking lot before disappearing back inside. As the door closed, I turned to face Hart—not the one I woke up with but the person I hurt in the past.

"Well, there you go, your master called you back. Guess old dogs can't learn new tricks." Her words dripped with resentment as she crossed her arms over her middle.

"Sweetheart—" I reached for her, only to miss when she stepped back away from me.

"Do you ever get tired of having that collar around your neck? One call, that's all it takes and you are gone again. Running back to your master like a bitch in heat." Her venomous words poured out.

"Listen to me. It's not like that; there is so much that you don't know." I was not above pleading with her to get her to hear me.

"So much I don't know? Really? Here's what I do know." Holding up one finger as she listed off her points, "You are loyal to no one but the Saints. You never completely committed to us because God forbid your precious Nicholas need you.

You had the chance to stay, and you didn't. You left, like always."

Ice settled in my vines. I was done. I re-lived the hurt I caused her daily. It played out repeatedly only changing out for the nightmare of my childhood before the Saints. My mind flashed the memories of arriving at Nicholas's family home. The adults spoke in hushed tones about how they were too late to save my parents. Then at the funeral, Nicholas's father spoke of my parents with affection and admiration. She may know me better than most, but with this she didn't know a *damn* thing.

"Be a good mutt and run home. Your master is waiting," she tossed over her shoulder as she walked away, her boots crunching on the gravel.

Fuck this.

Hart

I turned to create some distances between us because I was done with this conversation. All of a sudden I was whipped back around coming face to face with a seething V. He glared unblinkingly at me, the only movement being the visible rise and fall of his chest. "What the fu—" I went to spit in rage but was cut short.

"No, you've had your turn, now it's mine." I stood wide-eyed, his harsh tone startling me.

"I didn't run, *you* did. It wasn't me who built the walls between us, Hart. *You* carefully placed every brick to block me out. I will take some of the blame, but you checked out. *You*, Hart. I was left to bang on the outside. YOU.SHUT.ME.OUT. I have taken every hit, every cruel word, you and your brother threw at me. Listen to me carefully, Sweetheart, because you need to hear me loud and clear. I am done being the target for all your rage and hate. You want me to leave? You want me to be the villain? I'll be your villain; your wish is my command. I'm done." Standing to his full height, he released my arm, storming past me to the awaiting vehicle. I flinched at the sound of the door slamming.

The tires squealed and Diggs whipped the car out of the lot. Releasing a shaky breath, I move toward the shop. *I guess that's it.*

Coming down from the office, I sorted through the paperwork for the client pick-up. Running through my mental checklist, I made my way to the car before it rolled out. I popped the hood, deciding to start with the engine first. *It had to be this fucking car.*

I brought the hood down until it hovered open, before releasing it, allowing the weight to close it. The sound echoes around the shop V's words whisper through my mind. *"You shut me out."* The words came hushed, my ears being the only ones around to hear. "Rich coming from the one that kept secrets."

Moving to the rear of the car, I pulled the cleaning rag from my pocket to wipe the visible handprints away. *Who the fuck was leaning on this car?* It was V, the morning Diggs caught us. The embarrassment of being caught by my brother overshadowed what actually happened in that moment. Now, looking back, V had me wait to get out of the car. I heard everything they talked about, pieces coming back, something about *Lykos* and the *Keepers.* He made it clear that I need to stay put with the subtle shake of his head, right? Pursing my lips I stood staring at the smudged print. The car was getting detailed after lunch so that left me—glancing at the clock, damnit—roughly two hours to finish up. Pulling my phone out, I connected it to the shop speaker, clicking on a playlist and cranking it up. The voices in my head fading as the heavy beat consumed me.

Movement in my peripheral pulled my gaze up to the shop door. Signing off on the paperwork, I gave the crew a wave. "Just in time. She is ready for you guys to clean her up and make her shine." Stepping forward, Harold, the older man who led the crew, took the keys from my outstretched hand.

Chuckling, he said, "We just wash 'em' but we couldn't make them shine as bright as you."

"Oh, Harold, your words are as sweet as ever, but the pay is still the same." With a wink I turned to head up stairs to eat while they worked.

"Can't blame a man for trying." With a clap he started barking orders.

"Yea, yea." I laugh jokingly, walking back towards the office. My phone dings, pulling it out of my back pocket; it's a message from Diggs.

> "What in the world happened between you too?"

Another ding.

> "Whatever it was, could you not have waited until later to piss him off? Maybe not when we are getting ready to go handle something. I think you took it too far this time, Hart."

Rolling my eyes at Diggs and releasing a heavy sigh, I began to type, "Look—" Another message came through before I could finish typing.

> "Hey, we need to talk. Are you free to meet at brewed bean? -E"

I looked up at the clock, quickly typing out my response,

"Give me 10 and I'll be there."

I had about an hour before the customer should be here to pick up their car. This would also give me the opportunity to officially end things with him. Reaching the second floor, I walked over to the office, grabbing my keys and bag and heading to meet him. Things may be up in the air with V, but his words had been in my head all day. *Yay for hard talks.*

V

Pulling up to the abandoned two-story warehouse, Matt and I jump out, guns drawn. We hear shouting coming from the inside. *Something is not right.*

"He's supposed to be alone." Matt moves closer, lowering his voice to a whisper.

"Fuck, we need to get him out of here alive and take whatever prisoners we can for questioning." Matt nods, relaying the message through coms and waving to the others to move in.

Our bodies firmly pressed against the side of the building, stopping just before the open bay doorway, "Did you really think you could sneak away, and we wouldn't notice? You don't think we know what you've been up to?" I hold a finger up, motioning the men to wait. "All the questions, the missing files—" Looking around the corner, I see him kick the man on the ground in the face, and he lets out a groan. I turn back to Matt, "We need to move NOW!" signaling the Keepers to move, we storm the building. "Well— what do we have here?" The man who kicked our informant said with his arms up in a gesture to show he was not armed.

"I need you to back away from our guy." planting myself firmly.

"We were just playing with him a little." he spat out, "just some harmless fun, you could say." laughing, he circles the man still hunched over on the ground. They had done a number on him, and I'm unsure how much more he can take. "I mean, he isn't yours technically. Did you forget what family he serves?" Punctuating the statement with another kick to his battered body.

"I said back away." I take a step towards them, gun drawn.

"Alright, alright…" He slowly backs away, but I notice a slight nod to the guy on his right just as he takes off. I yell at my men, "Get the informant!" as guns start to sound off, "and capture anyone you can!" as I bolted after the man who gave the signal. Darting to the left, he takes off behind the concrete column, carefully making my way around the corner. Pausing, I check my blind spot as a bullet pings off the column next to my head. *Fuck! Too close.* I press my body closer to the pillar, "Come out, come out wherever you are…" he calls out in a sing-song voice. *This motherfucker is crazy.* Quickly, I come around the corner, shooting my shot just as a figure disappears through a doorway. Making my way to it, I hear Matt come across the com, "Target is secure and only one casualty. V, what is your position?"

Good. "Still in pursuit of the leader. I believe he is heading upstairs." rounding the corner, a metal pipe swung out, knocking the gun from my hands. Blindsided, I am tackled to the ground from behind, the pipe coming down across my back. "Motherfucker!" I grit out. *You're gonna regret that.*

Matt comes across the coms again, "Do you need backup?" Unable to respond, I hear a command come through, and they are headed in my direction. I roll, dodging the next blow, seeing my gun just out of reach. Slamming my boot into that bastard's knee, he drops down; taking that opportunity to get on my feet, I grab him by the collar and ram my knee into his face. Blood gushes out of his nose, pooling on the ground next to him. I pick up my gun, hovering it over his head, "Don't fucking move!" *Piece of shit.*

Matt and the Keepers round the corner about that time, "Get him ready. He's going first." With a nod, they haul him out of the corridor and back into the main area. Walking out with them, I see they have all but the one lifeless body tied up. Moving over to Diggs at the edge of the room, he squats next to the informant, speaking in a low voice. "When do you think they found you out?" Stepping closer, the beaten man raises his gaze to me.

"I don't know; I tried to be so careful when passing info along. He just doesn't give up. If I had a family, he would have tortured them to break me. That is why I turned.-" His left eye was swollen shut, the right barely opened as he turned back to Diggs. His face was streaked with blood and tears. "Most of what I gathered was from people who had the misfortune of working under him. He is a vile man. The things-"

Diggs interrupted the man, "Who is the man you are talking about? Was he here?

Releasing a slow breath before he spoke, looking around as if he expected the person to appear.

"No, but the men that were here will know where he is."

"What's his name?" Diggs, while usually calm with informants, was becoming agitated.

"I don't know his real name. Hell, it might be his name; it would be fitting." Looking back, he said, "Everyone in Lykos calls him Erebus."

Fuck.Fuck.Fuck

With a nod to Diggs, I stepped away to check in with Nicholas.

Pulling my phone out, I barely got the phone to my ear when his gruff voice answered,

"V."

"The Informant is secure, and Diggs is debriefing him now. They beat the shit out of him."

"*They? What do you mean, they?*" His words came out clipped. The noises around him were silenced. He was probably pacing his office as we spoke.

"When we got here, a group of Lykos scum were close to beating him to death. He will need a medical team, and so will a few of ours. We have taken the Lykos and will be questioning them. We did have one casualty." The line was quiet for a moment. Nicholas could not stand to lose people; it ate at him like the rest of us.

"Fuck!" He yelled through the phone, "Has he given you anything important?" I hoped he wasn't holding anything and he was alone.

Shifting to rest the phone on my other shoulder, I replied, "He was a blubbering mess when we got him. They really didn't want him to get away. He kept repeating that the Lykos family was making a move and that the target was a member of the Saints. Before you ask, no, he doesn't know who. We must notify all members to be on alert and move those who need it to a safe house." The line was quiet, but I knew better than to rush his reply. This made him a good leader—he processed the situation quickly before giving orders.

"Alright, I'll pass the word along. Anything else?" His voice sounded farther from the phone. The quick typing on his keyboard told me I was on speaker now.

"Yes, there was a name drop, *Erebus*." That fucking name filled me with rage and ice-cold dread. If he was connected to something, the body count rose. He showed no mercy when it came to his victims, whether they were a kill order or an innocent bystander.

Nicholas's voice came through as a low growl, "You're sure he said Erebus?" The clicking of his keys paused for my reply.

"Yeah, boss. He claims the guy that was wailing on him tonight would know where Erebus is." My phone vibrated against my ear. I pulled it away as an email notification popped up. The phone was quiet again before a loud crash rang from the other end. *Another bottle was lost to the wall. RIP, expensive whiskey.* Returning to the phone, I caught his irregular breathing before he slipped the chilly mask of indifference into place. This mask showed through as a calm leader on the outside, but I saw through it. Twenty-plus years of being attached at the hip would do that. His voice was strained, the tension bleeding into his tone. "This is a list of who needs to be moved. Diggs got it as well."

"Yeah, it just came through." Taking a page from Nicholas's book, I began to pace, needing to release some energy while waiting for his orders.

"V, we need his last known location. He needs to be brought in. Now. Question the leader that you caught tonight. Find out what he knows."

"Got it, boss!" Before I could disconnect the call, he spoke again.

"And V—" He paused before he finished his thought.

"Yea?"

"Be careful. Take a Keeper with you and watch your back." Releasing a frustrated breath, I accepted that we would have to engage with Erebus and other Lykos members. This was something we avoided when possible. Being on opposite ends in the Mafia world, we didn't see eye to eye. They were in the business of taking and hurting, whereas we chose to save and protect. Did we still get our hands dirty? Yes, but we saved more than we harmed.

Rejoining Diggs, I got his attention. "I'm taking Matt with me." Tilting his chin in acknowledgment, he tossed the keys to Matt.

"You should probably drive. I like the condition the car is currently in. Also, yes, I plan on checking on Hart." The corner of his lip tilted into a smirk. Flipping him the bird, I climbed into the passenger side. *Asshole.*

"Let's go."

Chapter Twelve

THE UNKNOWN

UNKNOWN

Sitting in a dark SVU across from the coffee shop, the blacked-out windows made it impossible for pedestrians to see who waited. She sat sipping on her coffee, clearly agitated, checking her phone every few minutes. Finishing her drink, she slid it away, before turning to look out the window. Checking her phone again, she stood and walked out visibly frustrated. The congested sidewalk allowed her to merge with the crowd of people. No matter, following her would be for the best.

Hart

"Are we still meeting?"

"Where are you?"

Unread

What the fuck? Slamming the shop door closed, I resisted the urge to hurl my phone across the shop. Harold's crew was just finishing up. Plastering a fake smile and approaching the now sparkling car, I thought, *Damn, she looks good.*

"Gorgeous, isn't she?" Harold asked.

Turning to face him, a genuine smile broke through, realizing he was talking to the man next to him about me. "Harold, you are a shameless flirt. But still the best detail man I know." Walking around the car, I admired just how stunning the car looked. As I made my way back to Harold, the door opened, and I glanced over my shoulder, noticing the owner walking in. *Perfect timing.*

Locking the door after Harold's team cleared out, I pulled my phone from my pocket, checking my messages again. *Nothing.* Not a single message from anyone. Pulling my earbuds out next and jamming them in my ears before connecting them. Music and cleaning were my methods of escaping. With the music handled, I turned to the shop. Grabbing a broom I started at the back of the shop working my way forward. With that completed, my workbench and tools were next. Pulling out the drawers one by one and doing the deep cleaning I had been putting off for a while, I set each tool aside for maintenance or for possible replacement. Once the tools were out, I began the tedious task of scrubbing the toolbox itself, drawers and all. The tools may be new, the toolbox was not. Diggs had bought it for me when I first said I wanted to work on cars. While wiping down the last drawer, I missed the cloth, running the palm of my hand along the sharp edge and slicing it open.

"FUUUCK!" My voice carried across the empty shop as blood immediately started to flow from my palm.

"Shit, shit, shit." Looking for a clean rag around me, I spotted the roll of blue shop towels. *That'll work.* The blood began to run down my arm, dripping onto the table, then the floor. Spinning around a little too quickly, my vision darkened around the edges. *Ooohh fuck.* Letting out a hiss of pain when my hip connected with the table, I sent some of the tools clattering to the floor. Deciding to forgo the paper towels, I started across the shop. Silver linings I guess, the shop had not been mopped and we had just gotten our tetanus shot boosters. *Small mercies.*

Not taking the time to pick up the tools, I started toward the sink, leaving a bloody trail in my wake. Quickly making my way over to the sink, I stumbled into a nearby tool cart, dumping everything in it onto the floor. *Shit, I'll have to clean that up later.*

Twisting the knobs on the sink, I stuck my hand under the stream. Crying out as the water set the one wound on fire. *Note to self, put a first aid kit by this sink.* I knew I would have to sterilize it. I kept my toolbox clean, but I did not need an infection from it. My music still blasted through my ears as I finished rinsing my palm. There was so much blood around the sink, making it look like a crime scene. Shutting the tap off, I reached for a wad of paper towels. Ripping them out of the holder, I started to pat my hand dry when a heavy hand landed on my shoulder, causing me to scream out.

Diggs

I burst through the door, my heart pounding in my ears. Hart had not answered her phone. V was also not answering. What a fucking prime time for them to go radio silent.

"HART!" She has to be here. She can't be gone. "HART!" Yelling again, I reached the steps. Bounding up them two at a time, I searched the top floor. "Damnit." I should have just told her everything. Coming back out of the office, my gaze snagged on something at Hart's station. Rushing down the stairs, I felt the blood drain from my face. I carefully approached the workbench, seeing blood and what looked like signs of a struggle. There was a bloody trail from one side of the shop to the other. So much blood. My sister's blood. Turning my head I vomited all over the floor. Snatching my phone from my pocket, I fired off a text to V.

"Hart is missing, there's blood everywhere."

Chapter Thirteen

THE SHAKEDOWN

V

I circled the chair that had been bolted to the floor in the center of the barren room. It was a struggle, but we finally got him, the notorious Erebus. I moved to stand before him, a hood over his head, his arms and legs secured to the chair with leather straps. "Did you really think we wouldn't know what y'all were up to?" We had been keeping tabs on the Lykos members for years now.

Our missions depended on knowing when other families were moving. If we failed to monitor them, the chances of getting people out unharmed were slim. Snatching the hood from his head, this fucker was going to talk. This may not be Erebus in the flesh, but he knew where that scumbag was. *Time for some persuasion.*

His lip tilted up in a knowing smile. Raring my fist back, I decked him before my mind could tell me it was a bad idea. Blood spewed from his nose. I definitely broke it.

"Motherfucker, you better start talking," I said, spitting the words in his face.

"Where is your sack of shit ringleader?" Silence.

Swinging my fist again, I connected with his jaw this time. His head lulled to the side, blood and spit running out of his mouth. "I got all night, asshole."

I usually left the shakedowns to Matt nowadays; this was personal. "Where should we start?" I looked the guy up and down before pulling my knife from my pocket. "Do you really want to lose vital parts for someone that doesn't give two shits about you?" This guy was a wannabe; years of experience told me that.

"My vote is an ear." Matt said from behind me, "He doesn't need both; one should do just fine... for now."

"True, true." putting on the act that I needed to weigh my options.

"Listen, listen, man, I don't know nothing." *Here we go.*

Coming to stand behind the man, I let the knife rest on his shoulder, his fear skyrocketing at the close proximity. "Could do an eye. That's also another thing he only needs one of." He tapped the blade on his shoulder.

"You really are too generous. Offering to leave him at least one of everything. I mean, he should also have two balls." Stepping forward, Matt placed his boot at the guy's crotch and ground the heel of his boot in.

"FUCK, STOP STOP I'LL FUCKING TALK..-" He wailed in pain as Matt pulled his boot away. *Well, damn, that was easy.* "It was all a distraction. They had caught on to the mole long before now. They knew you wanted him, so they used that against you. You sanctimonious asshole will do anything to -" he let out a blood-curdling scream as I slice through his ear. WHAT THE FUCK?!"

"Damn, who would have thought losing an ear could make you an even more ugly son of a bitch." *This is why I brought Matt. Like myself, he was good* at pushing people to the limit by talking.

"Where the fuck is Erebus?" stepping back in front of the guy, I snarled. "He got called to one of the main houses. H-he was going to pick up that little saint bitch he has been fucking but had to get his other guys to. Wish I would have been with them." This guy really needed to learn when to shut up. "I mean, Erebus has been talking about that sweet pussy for a month. Said that once he was done, she was fair ga-" Placing the blade at his neck had him biting his words back.

"My guy, you have ROOYALLLLYY fucked up. That woman you just disrespected-." Before Matt could finish his statement, My phone chirped with a text message. I had ignored the call and previous message.

"Message from your little wolf?" His voice was raspy as he turned to spit more blood on the floor. This piece of shit knew who Hart was to me. He was fucking baiting me but still trying to save his own ass by giving us info.

Pulling the phone from my pocket, I scanned the screen. My veins turned to ice at the message, and the noise around me muffled like I had cotton in my ears. Hysterical laughter broke through my haze. "Damn, what I would have given to have been on that pick-up team." Matt's fist connects with his face, only shutting him up momentarily. "She would have been a nice fuck. I'm sure they will treat her well until Erebus gets there."

In two steps, I had my hand wrapped around his throat. "Where the fuck is *she*?" Giving his throat a squeeze.

"No, Clue again, I wasn't on that team. Erebus did say that she is a submissive little whore. Hopefully, that will help her out, and she won't be too loo—" His words were cut off by the hit to the side of his head, knocking him out cold. *This guy is a fucking idiot.*

I hit the call button, and Diggs answered on the first ring. "Erebus was her fucking boyfriend. Trace that number and stay at the Cathedral, I am on my way now." I disconnected the call, catching the keys Matt tossed me as he said, "Go, I got this." Moving towards the car, I called, "He lives until I find her."

V

I throw the door open to the car, and I run to where Digg's stands at the open bay door. "Where the fuck is Hart?" I yelled, pushing past him. My eyes bounce around the space. There is blood from one end of the shop to the other. Tools that I assume are her's are scattered around one of the tables and her bench. *What the hell happened? Why would they take Hart? Fuck! I shouldn't have left her.*

"She isn't here, V. I have called and messaged her. Nothing. The number you sent is Erebus. I'm waiting for a location ping now. Have you called Nicholas?" Diggs' voice pulls me back to reality.

"Why would they take Hart?" I ask the question that has been plaguing me.

"There are things you don't know. Things that even Hart doesn't know. I haven't been able to tell her much because it's not just my story." He replies as his phone dings with a message.

"Well seems like now would be a prime fucking time to tell me, Diggs." I stare at him as he types out a reply to whoever the fuck is texting him. My anger grew as he continued to type. "DIGGS! GET OFF YOUR FUCKING PHONE!" I crowded into his space, snatching the phone from his hand.

"Listen here, asshole. I get that you are spiraling, but the person messaging is a friend who has found Erebus. I was sending it to one of the teams to pick his ass up." Diggs snapped back, grabbing the phone and shoving past me. "Ya know what? Fuck you! Fuck you, Valentine. You don't think I am going out of my mind not knowing where she is? She is my sister, jackass. MY. FUCKING. FAMILY. I don't have much family left. So back the fuck up." By the end of his rant, we were standing chest to chest. A throat cleared behind me.

Whipping around, I drew my gun at the same time. "Who the hel-"

"Put that away, big fella. Diggs asked me to come. I was here earlier with Hart." Harold, the Cathedral's main detail man, under the table also did clean up when we needed it. The man was damn good at what he did.

"Sorry, Harry." I lowered the gun as my adrenaline began to waver.

"It's ok, Tiny. Emotions are high. I told Diggs already; the crew and I had cleared out before your girl left." He walked over towards us, patting my arm as he passed, heading towards the back of the shop. Harold had been with the Saints longer than I had been alive. While Nicholas had always been like my brother, Harold played pseudo-grandfather to most kids who grew up near the core family.

Pulling the hair tie from my falling bun, I ran my fingers through the tangled strands, tugging in frustration. *I have to find her. I can't lose her. I won't accept losing her.*

"Diggs, ping her location again." tying my hair back up to stop myself from ripping it out.

"It still shows that her phone is here. I have looked everywhere." Turned his phone to show me the small blinking dot. It couldn't give a precise location, but her phone was in the shop.

"Call it again." I turn toward Hart's bench. When nothing happened, I looked back to check Diggs was, in fact, calling. Shaking the lit phone, I looked back to the work area. *Was that..?*

"Diggs, call it again," I said, walking over. *Fuck.* Getting down on my stomach, I shifted the tools that had fallen during the struggle to reveal Hart's phone. Damn, the screen was shattered again. She can be pissed, but I will be buying her a new phone after this. New phone, new case, headphones, whatever the fuck she wants, I'll give it to her. Standing, I carry the phone back to Diggs, "It must have gotten lost in the shuffle. The screen is shattered. Is there any way to recover what was on it?" I ask before passing it off. With a nod, Diggs turned and walked upstairs to the office.

"She'll be ok, Tiny," Harold spoke from behind me, startling me.

My voice sounded small, even to my ears. Once again, I was a small, scared child looking at the adults around me. "Harry, I'm scared I have lost her." Wiping my hand down my face, I covered my eyes. "I can't"

"Do you remember the first time we met?"

The older man reached over, tapping my elbow.

"How could I forget someone buying me ice cream?" I snickered.

Harold leans against the motorcycle lift, "I had gone to my super-secret spot at the main house, only to be met with a sad kid."

"It was a broom closet, Harry… Not that big of a super-secret spot." moving to prop beside him on the lift.

"Meh, you thought it was a good spot then. Well, either way, sad kids made young me nervous. So, how do you make a sad kid happy?" He cut his eyes over, "Take them for ice cream."

"And my reply, are you kidnapping me?" I might have been a sad kid, but I was not stupid. I knew how the darker parts of the world ran. It's how I ended up in the closet at the Saint's house, missing my parents but not wanting anyone to see me weak. I have never told Harold what that meant to me. How those trips to get ice cream or sweets made a difference. After that, the first time, Harold always seemed to be there, where I needed to not be the sad orphan living with the Saints. He would brush it off as he just happened to be there, but I knew the Saints would call him. After that first time, I returned happier and lighter, and that was what they cared about, the kids getting to be kids.

"I never thanked you for all the times you did that for me." My tone was low and rough as I spoke.

"No need to thank me, Tiny. I needed it, too. I was mad at the world and needed something to focus on. Seeing you happy made me happy." Looking down, the corn of his mouth tipped into a soft smile.

A loud bang caused us both to jump, Diggs was running down the stairs. "She was meeting him! They were meeting at the Brewed Bean. We get him, we get her." Diggs spoke in a rush, crossing over to us. "Harold, you good to clean and lock up?"

"Yeah, go get our girl." pushing at my arm. *I'm coming, Sweetheart. I'm coming.*

V

Speeding down the winding roads, I didn't know where I was really headed. All I knew was that I needed to find her. How could I have been so stupid not to check in with her after learning what the Lykos family was up to. *I let my damn pride get in the way.* The way we left things this morning— that can't be the last—I *needed* to find her. Picking up my phone, I hit Nicholas on the speed dial and he answered on the first ring. "V—" I cut him off before he could say anything else.

"They have her, Nick! They fucking took her!" In a panic, I began word vomiting everything I just found out. Banging the palm of my hand on the steering wheel, I cried, "That fucking bastard Erebus was her boyfriend. He's been playing us all along, and now they have her.

"How could I have been so blind? I should have known something like this would happen. I fucking knew that guy was trouble." I should have beat the shit out of him the day he came to the shop. "Nicholas, I can't lose her. She is and has been everything to me. I will burn everyth—"

"V!" He shouts from the other end of the line, stopping my nearly incoherent rambling. "Calm the fuck down. Hart is with me and Alessandra at your place." There was no way that was right. There had been blood everywhere. That bastard said someone else got to her.

Straining to force the words out, the low rasp that followed came as a whisper, "Diggs was correct; blood was all over the Cathedral, and it looked like there had been a struggle." She was hurt. I should have stayed. Why didn't I stay? *Fuck.*

"Valentine, she cut her hand. She is fine—" His voice faded a bit, speaking in hushed tones as if he were talking to someone else in the background. "Just get your ass here."

"Yeah, I... I'm coming, tell her I'm coming." I disconnected the call and tossed the phone in the passenger seat.

She is safe. She is safe. They are at my house and she is safe. Fuck, I could have lost her. Repeating the words like a mantra was the only peace I had the whole drive. Everything was taking too long, the cars moving too slow, lights turning at the wrong time. When I pulled up to my place, my hands ached from how tightly I had gripped the steering wheel.

She is safe. She is safe.

"I know you want to go in and see your sister, but I need you to handle getting Erebus to a secure location." My words came out far calmer than I felt. "I will tell her to call, and in the morning, we will trade out, and I will handle our little problem." Turning to look at him, the set of his jaw showed he did not like this plan, but if it was for Hart, he would do it.

"Okay. I will ask Alessandra to come in the morning, too. I have kept it from everyone, but they deserve to know before anyone else." *Again with the cryptic bullshit.*

My heart was beating out of my chest when I reached the door. Throwing the door open, I searched the room, feeling as feral as I probably looked. Everything in me screamed to find her, see with my own eyes she was here. When Nicholas stepped in my line of sight, the leash that had been holding my control snapped.

"Get the fuck out of my way," I roared at the man I considered my brother.

"Val." His hands raised in surrender trying to placate me. "Listen to me, you have got to calm down. Take a breath. She is safe. Do you hear me? Hart is safe. Watch me, Valentine." His chest rose, taking a deep breath, wanting me to mimic him. Forcing air through my nose, my lungs filled for the first time since receiving Diggs's text.

"There you are. Alessandra is with her, helping her get cleaned up and changed." Giving me a once over, he added, "I suggest you do the same before you see her."

With my body coming down, I became hyper aware of just how I looked. Specks of blood dotted my shirt and pants. Between saving the informant, finding that piece of shit Erebus, and then the interrogation, I looked rough. My head fell forward, the sweaty strands of hair falling loose around my face. He was right. *As always.*

"Ok." My voice was a whisper.

Nicholas stepped to my side, his palm

gently landing between my shoulder blades. The warmth from his palm reached my chilled skin. He knew I was coming down, and this was his way of grounding me to the now. While I was the muscle for the Saints that most feared, when I came down from an adrenaline high, all the demons from my past would claw their way in. Learning this the hard way after a particularly rough mission, the situation hit a little too close to home. When Nicholas found me at rock bottom, my darkness was consuming me. We weren't kids, but also not adults. That was the day he earned his nickname from me—*St. Nick*, gifting me some strength in my time of need. Just like I had seen him at his lowest, he had also seen me.

"Shower first." He nudged me through the bathroom door. "I have ordered food and it should be here—" His words were cut off by the buzzer. "Now." Pausing, his eyes scanned my face, his brow creasing with worry.

"Go on, St. Nick, I apparently need to shower."

A low chuckle came as he turned,

muttering "Dumbass" under his breath.

V

Steam poured from the bathroom as I opened the door, stepping into the hall. With the girls taking the master bathroom, it left me in the spare. Thankfully, Nicholas had grabbed clean sweats for me as I showered, placing them on the sink. While showers worked in a pinch, I enjoyed the oversized tub that was the main attraction of the ensuite. Now was not the time to be soaking.

Hearing muffled voices, I turned towards the living room, spotting Nicholas and Alessandra, but not Hart. Reaching them in a few short steps, I was mct with Alessandra wrapping her tiny arms around me. While she had not been in our lives long, she was family. I gave her back a light pat as Nicholas cleared his throat. Releasing me, she stepped back to his side.

"Hart is in the tub in your bathroom. We are going to get out of your hair." He wrapped an arm around his Vixen and kissed the top of her head.

"Thank you for taking care of her."

When I didn't.

"Stop. You did nothing wrong. I know that I scared her at the shop, and for that I am sorry, but I would never risk her safety. Once Vixen was with me, I headed to pick up Hart. She was heading to the coffee shop. I didn't want to disturb her, so we just watched over her, then picked her up at the shop. You are my brother, I always have your back." *And I had his.*

"I put the food in the fridge, but I took some water bottles to the bedroom." Alessandra added. "And snacks. You know, in case you guys don't want to get up." Her cheeks pinked with a blush, realizing how her words sounded.

"Careful, I can't have you playing Cupid. You would definitely put me out of a job." With a chuckle I added, "Besides, Cupid Saint just doesn't have the same ring to it." I shot Nicholas a pointed stare.

"And on that note." He turned her to the door, flipping me off instead of a wave, and they left me standing in my living room. *Now to find my Sweetheart.*

Hart

Relaxing into the warm water of the tub, bubbles came up to my chest, an endless supply of them because of the jets. Sliding under the water, the gentle whoosh of the water jets soothed me, as I quieted the noise from tonight's events. Breaking the surface, I was greeted by the sight of V leaning against the edge of the tub. Reaching over, he brushed my hair away from my face. Catching his hand, I brought it to my lips, placing a soft kiss on his palm. I could see there was a fire burning behind his eyes.

"I thought I'd lost you tonight," he said in a low growl, emotion lacing his words. "I thought I'd never see you again, *Mia.*" His eyes traced over my face, taking in every detail.

"Sweets…? Look at me, I'm ok. Nicholas told me a little of what was going on, but I want to hear it from you." Leaning my cheek into his hand, I took in his features. His eyes were alert; the usual lightness they carried was not present. *I can fix that.*

Sliding my hand to grip his wrist, I began to guide his hand down. A spark of recognition caused him to hesitate.

"Sweets." I was not above begging. "Please, I need you."

His pupils were blown, leaving only a sliver of color around the edges. *There he is.* His hand began to move.

"So needy, baby." He reached up to one of my nipples, tweaking it until it hardened, causing a moan to slip from my lips. He moved, showering the other with the same attention before traveling lower. His palm cupped my center. "Is this where it hurts?" he asked, applying more pressure.

Sliding one finger between my folds and grazing my clit sent a shock of pleasure through me. "It hurts so bad, make it go away please." I moaned as his finger slipped inside. This was always how we found each other—words and talking would come, but we connected with touch. Getting lost in each other, giving the other what they needed. With slow movements, he worked his finger in and out, pulling my climax from deep inside me.

"I won't make you wait, Sweetheart. I need this as much as you do." His mouth rested by my ear. "Do you know how close you were to being taken away from me?" Grinding his palm against my clit.

"You could never lose me, Sweets." I turned to kiss his jaw, before letting out a whimper when he stroked over that little bundle of nerves, pulling out to add a second finger. "Valentine, yes."

"That's right. You. Are. Mine. This greedy pussy is mine," he said, punctuating his words with a thrust of his finger. "You are so slick and tight." My walls pulsed around his fingers. "God, you feel so good clenching around my fingers." Pumping in and out a few times, he removed his fingers. "I have an idea, baby." Droplets of water fell as he reached, turning the lever to divert water to the handheld faucet.

"Are you ready to be a good girl and cum?" *Fuck yes.* My knees rested open against the sides of the tub as the head broke the water's surface.

"I'm going to need your help. Can you do that?" he asked, guiding one of my hands to wrap around the faucet. "Hold it right here." With that he angled the stream at my sensitive clit.

"Oh fuck, yes, yes. I'm so close. Please make me cum." I whimpered, my pleas coming out on a broken moan when his fingers plunged back in. My climax roared to life, with the water pounding away at my swollen clit. With only a few pumps, my stomach tightened as my legs shook, waiting for permission. Leaning in, V ran his lips up my neck before his words ghosted over my ear. "Come for me, *Sweetheart.*" With that I shattered. Shaking as wave after wave of pleasure rolled over me, my mouth fell open on a silent scream, before slumping, letting the wand slip from my hand. Removing his hand, he grabbed the shampoo, pouring a dollop into his hand.

"You don't have to do that." My head rested on the tub's edge, my heavy lids falling closed.

"Yes, I do. I want to take care of you." Speaking in a low voice, he continued, "I need to take care of you." He worked the shampoo through my hair, massaging my scalp.

"Mmm, that feels amazing." I immediately relaxed into his touch, my words coming out slow and a little slurred. Rinsing my hair he moved to my body, lovingly running a washcloth over my body, changing to the other side to be able to reach everywhere. When he saw my bandaged hand, he dropped the rag, sucking in a breath before carefully inspecting the wrappings.

"I'm so sorry you got hurt. I shouldn't have left that way," he choked out.

"Sweets, this was not your fault. I was mad, yes, and I was rage cleaning but not because of you." I waited for him to meet my gaze. "I received a message from the guy I was seeing." His body stiffened, and he went to pull his hand back. Grabbing it back, I said, "No, don't pull away, let me finish." I winced but needed him to hear me. "I was going to tell him that we were done. I didn't know, V, I swear. Nicholas told me who he was. I was so worried about you." His face softened at my words, but I had more to say. "I didn't know where we stood, but staying with him was not an option. You are who I want. Do you hear me? *You*. We will fight and drive each other mad, but you're it for me. I'm done trying to find better when the best has my heart already." Shifting to my knees, I took his mouth in a kiss. His hands moved around to grip my ass. He stood with a grunt, taking me with him as I caught a glimpse of his bruised and beaten back in the mirror. "Oh my god, V!" I try to wiggle my way out of his arms, "let me go so I can look at you!" His grip tightens on my ass, "I'm fine." he says, leaning in closer "You should see the other guy." a smirk playing across his lips as they reach mine. We continued to kiss as my body slid down his until my feet rested on the warm tile.

Turning to grab a fluffy towel, he carefully dried me off. With that done, he picked me up bridal style, carrying me to his bedroom. As he carefully laid me on the bed, I realized he had pulled the covers down prior to coming into the bathroom. His gaze trailed down my body, landing on the tattoo that covered a good portion of my thigh. He trailed his fingertips across the ink, causing goosebumps to raise.

"This is new. What's the story?" he asked, taking in every small detail of the tattoo.

"I got it after we ended the last time. You're not the only one to use ink for therapy." A small smile crossed my lips. "I was so mad at you. When I left, my anger faded fast, turning into guilt and sadness. I wanted to blame you for everything, but I couldn't. I shut you out. I had my tattoo artist draw this up. The wing and arrow are for you, my cupid. While the roses are pink because of the pink roses you always brought me. The skull was because I was being dramatic about being heartbroken." A little giggle slipped out. "If I couldn't have you, I wanted something that reminded me of you." My eyes glazed over with tears.

"Oh, Sweetheart." He reached quickly to wipe his eyes before dropping his damp sweats and climbing into bed with me. He pulled me into his chest. Feeling warm and safe in his arms, my eyes began to fall closed.

"Stay with me," my words muffled against his chest.

"Always, Sweetheart." His words reached me as I drifted off to sleep.

I love you, sweets.

Chapter Fourteen

THE MEETUP

V

Waking up with Hart's warm body pressed to me was the definition of heaven. She had rolled over in her sleep, snuggling back until that perfect ass was right against me. *Down, boy. We don't have time.* Right now. Not wanting to disturb her—she looked so peaceful—but I had some unfinished business that needed to be handled. Gently I worked my arm out from underneath her until she started to stir. *Shit.*

"Where are you going? Come back to bed."

"I wish I could, sweetheart, but there is something I need to handle." She let out a huff. "Diggs and Alessandra will be heading this way in a bit. Rest as long as you need, and I'll meet you at the shop soon." I leaned down and kissed her on the forehead.

Catching my arm before I could turn to walk away, she said, "Sweets—" I leaned in closer. "Be careful." She grabbed the back of my neck pulling me in for a kiss as she whispered, "I love you." Closing the distance, our lips met in a fierce kiss. Her words washed over me like a soothing balm. The pieces of my heart sliding back into place. Finally.

"I love you, Sweetheart."

V

Tucking my helmet under my arm, the metal door groaned as I pulled it open. I had called Matt on the way to fill him in. My eyes slowly adjusted to the dimly lit room, a figure hanging where he was strung up by his wrist. *Perfect.*

Matt approached, whipping his blood-stained hands with a rag. "He's a tough one, that guy." he chuckled, "Motherfucker doesn't want to give anything away. I think he needs a firmer hand."

Reaching down, I grabbed the bucket of water and threw the contents directly at his face. "Wakey, wakey!" Jolting awake, Erebus groaned in pain before his eyes shot wide. "You know I'm a little disappointed in you." taunting him as I walked over to the med cart Matt conveniently left, "Matt took it easy on you, and you not only broke but also pissed yourself." Shaking my head as I circled him, listening to his pathetic moans, I reached for the scalpel. "People may be scared of you until they meet Matt. He is so creative, isn't he?" Coming to stand in front of him, I place the blade against his cheek, dragging it slowly down his face.

"Then again, I did train him." I bring the tip to his chest, digging it deep into the muscle. He cries out in agony, "Damn, it stopped. Must have hit bone." releasing a sarcastic laugh, I jerk the blade free. "Hmmmm... maybe I need to try a different spot." slicing the blade across his abdomen.

"Please..." his pleading moans growing louder.

"I'm sorry... What was that? I can't hear

you without your tongue." silently, I nod at Matt. He grabs Erebus by the hair of his head, snatching it back, forcing his mouth open, giving me better access. I reach in, pull his tongue out, gripping it tightly, and begin to slice away at it. Matt releases his grip on Erebus as his screams echo off the barren walls around us,

"Oh come on now... It's not that bad, is it?" I placed the scalpel back on the tray and waited for his response, though I knew one wouldn't come.

" Cat got your tongue?" My tone mocking his current situation.

Clapping my hands together, I said, "Well, unfortunately, your time with us has come to an end." I pulled my gun from its holster, using the barrel to tilt his head up. I continued, "Oh, and by the way... Hart is safe in my bed, in case you'd like to know." pressing the weapon to his forehead.

As I clicked the safety off, he tried to speak, "Plea—" The shot rang out through the building. *Good riddance.*

Hart

Dragging myself from bed was harder than usual, but when Diggs and Alessandra arrived with coffee and breakfast, I willingly left it. When we got to the Cathedral, the evidence of my chaos had been erased. *Thank God.*

"Yep, once again I was left to clean up your mess. Just glad I wasn't met with V's naked ass this time." I knew what he was trying to do—seeing the shop had rattled him. Diggs had always been protective of me, constantly watching over me and keeping me out of trouble.

"Why would you not want to look at his ass? It's a great ass," I shot back.

As he shook his head, we climbed the stairs and walked to sit at the long conference table, digging into our breakfast. Breaking the comfortable silence, my brother cleared his throat before speaking. "So we need to talk."

I shot a quick glance to Alessandra trying to gauge if she knew what this was about. She looked as lost as me. "What's wrong, *Bichito?*" The childhood nickname slipping out. Diggs hated it, but he told me a story once about our parents—not the people who raised us but our biological parents. Our mother had always called him Bichito, which meant 'little bug'. It was one of the only times he cracked and told me anything.

"Nothing is wrong. I just should have told you this a long time ago. Both of you." He looked between us. "Alessandra, there was a reason I knew you had a peanut allergy. You are my and Mia's cousin." He paused, giving her a moment to process before he continued.

"Your mother Deyanira Lykos is our aunt by marriage. We were very young when your father helped to get us away from the Lykos family. When we arrived with the Saints, they had to split us up because the family wasn't prepared for three kids. Your father didn't want you connected to the Saints, so the family that took you in was just under the protection of the family, while Mia and I went to a lower-level family within the family." Taking a breath he forged on.

"The day we got out didn't go as planned. When we went to the meeting spot, it had been compromised. Alessandra, your dad sacrificed himself so we could get away." Reaching my hand over, I took her hand as silent tears tracked down her cheeks.

"You were both so small but so strong. He told me to take the two of you, run and don't look back. So I did just that, I went to where he had told me. It was to a Saint's safe house. They took us in, but when we separated us, they wouldn't tell me anything about where they sent you, Alessandra. I tried, I begged them to let you stay with us, but it's not what your dad wanted." His voice strained, tears now running down his face. "I'm so sorry—I let them separate us."

Alessandra began to shake her head, reaching her other hand across to Diggs. "No, you have nothing to apologize for. You were just a child, like we were." Giving his hand a squeeze, she said, "We have each other now." A gentle knock on the collapsed glass panel interrupted us. "Knock, knock." V stood holding a large bouquet of pink roses in one hand and Milo's leash in the other. *My boys.*

Milo pulled on his leash until V relented,

allowing him to run and jump into my lap, showering my tear-soaked face with kisses. As I craned my neck up to look at V, he placed a chaste kiss on my lips. "Hey Beautiful. Miss us?"

"Always."

"Can you all just get a room? Damn, V and Mia had sex in a client car, and now y'all are being all fucking lovey dovey." My brother, the comedian. Alessandra snorted with laughter, causing a domino effect, the rest of us joining in.

Nicholas

Heading out the door of my office to the Cathedral, my phone started to ring. Pulling it out of my pocket, I answered, "Hello." My body tensed, every sense immediately on high alert.

"Nicholas—" A woman's tone comes through. "We haven't met before, but my name is—" My posture stiffens at the recognition of her voice.

"I know exactly who you are, Deyanira Lykos," I said, cutting her off.

"Good. So, we can skip the pleasantries then. You have taken something very important to me," she said snidely.

"If you're talking about that bastard Erebus, then yea I have him. Or I should say I did." V handled that little problem this morning. We had gotten all the information we could out of him, and after what he did to Hart, he deserved it. I gladly let V dish out the final punishment.

"You see, I thought that might have happened," she said as if I really cared.

"And let me guess, you had a contingency set-in place?"

"Why, yes, I did. You see, I thought it only fair to take something equally as important to you."

"Have you heard from all of your Keepers lately? Maybe a particular one whose family owns—"

No, the fuck she didn't.

"Now what was it again? Oh yes, King's Bakery?"

"You bitch! If it's a war you want, it's a war you will get." I ended the call, quickly making my way out the door, calling everyone to get eyes on Angel.

V

Coming through the door, Nicholas stared down at his screen. His face was pale, hands shaking slightly from how hard he was gripping the device. "Nicholas." He looked up meeting my gaze. Hearing his name, Alessandra rose, walking into his open arms. Leaning down he kissed the top of her head before whispering something in her ear. Burying her face in his chest, a soft muffled whimper accompanied the gentle sobs that shook her small form.

"Nicky…" A sense of dread knotted my stomach.

"Angel has been shot…"

THE END

Names & Meanings

Alessandra- Greek for defender of men

Bichito- Spanish for little bug

Deyanira- Greek for capable of
great destruction

Erebus-Greek for darkness

Hart- German for deer

Lykos- Greek for wolf

Valentine- Scottish for strong,
healthy, brave & rule

This story was a product of friendship,
perseverance, & a love for smutty books.
You wanted more…
We gave you more…
Hope you love it!

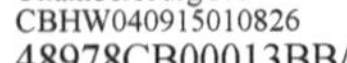